Blade

Also From Alexandra Ivy

Also From Laura Wright

Eternal Blood (Especial)
Eternal Captive
Eternal Beast
Eternal Beauty (Especial)
Eternal Demon
Eternal Sin

BAYOU HEAT SERIES
Raphael & Parish
Bayon & Jean-Baptiste
Talon & Xavier
Sebastian & Aristide
Lian & Roch
Hakan & Severin
Angel & Hiss
Michel & Striker
Rage & Killian
Ice & Reaux

WICKED INK CHRONICLES *(New Adult Series- 17+)*
First Ink
Shattered Ink
Rebel Ink

CAVANAUGH BROTHERS
Branded
Broken
Brash
Bonded

MASTERS OF SEDUCTION
Volume One
Masters Of Seduction Two

INCUBUS TALES

SPURS, STRIPES and SNOW Series
Sinful in Spurs

Blade

A Bayou Heat Novella

By Alexandra Ivy & Laura Wright

1001 Dark Nights

EVIL EYE
CONCEPTS

Blade
A Bayou Heat Novella
By Alexandra Ivy & Laura Wright

1001 Dark Nights
Copyright 2017 Debbie Raleigh & Laura Wright
ISBN: 978-1-945920-31-8

Foreword: Copyright 2014 M. J. Rose
Published by Evil Eye Concepts, Incorporated

Acknowledgments from the Authors

We would like to thank, from the bottom of our hearts, the two fearless leaders of 1001 Dark Nights, Liz Berry and MJ Rose. They welcomed us into their family, and we have come to adore the whole tribe. Thank you so much to our editors, cover artists, PR wonders and formatters! You are angels from heaven!

And of course, as always, we would be nothing without our readers. You make us excited to get to the laptop each day. May you love the Pantera forever. Just as we do.

Sign up for the 1001 Dark Nights Newsletter
and be entered to win a Tiffany Key necklace.

There's a contest every month!

Go to www.1001DarkNights.com to subscribe.

As a bonus, all subscribers will receive a free
1001 Dark Nights story
The First Night
by Lexi Blake & M.J. Rose

One Thousand and One Dark Nights

Once upon a time, in the future...

*I was a student fascinated with stories and learning.
I studied philosophy, poetry, history, the occult, and
the art and science of love and magic. I had a vast
library at my father's home and collected thousands
of volumes of fantastic tales.*

*I learned all about ancient races and bygone
times. About myths and legends and dreams of all
people through the millennium. And the more I read
the stronger my imagination grew until I discovered
that I was able to travel into the stories... to actually
become part of them.*

*I wish I could say that I listened to my teacher
and respected my gift, as I ought to have. If I had, I
would not be telling you this tale now.
But I was foolhardy and confused, showing off
with bravery.*

*One afternoon, curious about the myth of the
Arabian Nights, I traveled back to ancient Persia to
see for myself if it was true that every day Shahryar
(Persian: شهریار, "king") married a new virgin, and then
sent yesterday's wife to be beheaded. It was written
and I had read, that by the time he met Scheherazade,
the vizier's daughter, he'd killed one thousand
women.*

Something went wrong with my efforts. I arrived in the midst of the story and somehow exchanged places with Scheherazade – a phenomena that had never occurred before and that still to this day, I cannot explain.

Now I am trapped in that ancient past. I have taken on Scheherazade's life and the only way I can protect myself and stay alive is to do what she did to protect herself and stay alive.

Every night the King calls for me and listens as I spin tales. And when the evening ends and dawn breaks, I stop at a point that leaves him breathless and yearning for more. And so the King spares my life for one more day, so that he might hear the rest of my dark tale.

As soon as I finish a story... I begin a new one... like the one that you, dear reader, have before you now.

Chapter 1

It was the prickle on the back of his neck that warned Blade he was being followed.

Slowing his steps, he forced himself into a casual stroll as he checked out the streets of Bonne, Louisiana. He feigned interest in several glass storefronts that lined the town square, nodding toward the occasional pedestrian who studied him with blatant curiosity—and if he wasn't mistaken—which he rarely was—a thread of fear.

Clearly, the small town thirty miles south of Baton Rouge didn't get many visitors.

Of course, it was possible that the men stared because he was six foot four with the hard muscles of a trained athlete that flexed and rippled beneath his faded jeans and ivory thermal shirt. And the women...well, their gazes were clearly trained on his short gold hair, midnight eyes, finely chiseled features, and those wide lips that normally smiled with a charming ease, but were now pressed together with grim determination.

Turning onto a side street, he thankfully found it all but deserted. The town had obviously never been a bustling metropolis, but over the years it'd faded to a sleepy village. Which meant he could deal with his stalker without unwanted attention.

Maintaining his leisurely saunter, he passed by an abandoned gas station that was next to an empty lot. The breeze tugged at his short hair, chilling his skin.

Louisiana had two seasons. Hot and humid. Or cool and humid.

Today it was the latter.

Come on, my friend, he mused to the male who was tailing him. *Just another couple of blocks and we can...chat.*

At the edge of town, it didn't slowly ease from commercial to residential to suburbs like most places. It just ended. As if the thick woods ahead of him refused to give way to progress.

Turning, his back to the stand of trees now, he folded his arms over his chest and studied the seemingly empty street.

"Show yourself, Hiss," he commanded in a low voice.

The male emerged from the side of a small church with peeling paint and a steeple that tilted at a precarious angle.

He was easily as big as Blade, with black hair that had grown long and shaggy over the past two months. His eyes were dark gray, but as the late afternoon sunlight splashed over them, there was a glimmer of amber deep in their depths. An indication that Hiss's puma had enjoyed the hunt.

Both men were Pantera, a mystical race of puma shifters who lived in the depths of the Louisiana swamps, in a once-hidden community called the Wildlands. Created by twin Goddesses, they were creatures who were neither human or animal, but a mixture of the two. Faster and stronger than normal humans, their senses were hyper-acute. And when surrounded by the magic of their homelands they were capable of shifting into pumas.

Over the past year they'd battled the dying magic of the Wildlands, exposure of their kind, and a group of humans, led by Christopher Benson, who were determined to use the Pantera's magical blood for their own profit.

No longer were they safely hidden behind their magic. Everything and everyone was suspect—the lives of their kind always hanging in the balance.

"Hello, Blade."

"Sloppy," Blade drawled at the Suit. "I picked up your scent as soon as you entered town."

Hiss shrugged. "I started following you over an hour ago."

"An hour?" Blade's brows snapped together. "Seriously?" That meant Hiss had been behind him since he'd left New Orleans and jogged his way north.

He could have driven to Bonne, but he was searching for a particular scent. He hadn't wanted to risk missing it.

"Not so sloppy, eh?" Hiss demanded, his lips curving into a smirk.

Blade felt a jolt of anger. Not at Hiss, but at himself. What the hell was his problem? How could he have been so careless? He better than anyone understood the necessity of being constantly on guard. Fuck. Hadn't he already paid a high enough price for his stupid, arrogant assumptions that he was invincible?

"No, it's creepy," he snapped. Later, he would beat himself up for letting Hiss make a fool of him. Right now he just wanted to know why the male had tracked him from New Orleans. "Don't you have a new mate to stalk?"

Blade had been in one of the basement cells of Benson's lab with Hiss when the older male had found the female destined to be his mate.

Hiss's expression softened. "I do, and I'm pissed as hell that I'm not currently making her purr with pleasure."

"Not as pissed as I am that you've been following me," Blade countered. "What do you want?"

"A chat."

Blade sneered. He'd been off the radar for weeks, which meant that Hiss had devoted a lot of time and effort to finding him.

No one did that just for a chat.

Hell, they were Pantera males. Chatting was bullshit.

"I don't have time for this," he said.

"You can talk to me or you can talk to Raphael." Hiss shrugged. "Your choice."

Blade grimaced. Raphael was the head of the Suits, which was the diplomatic faction of the Pantera. Since Blade was also a Suit, that meant Raphael was his leader. And among the Pantera, "leader" wasn't an empty title. It meant that Raphael gave orders, and then kicked ass when they weren't obeyed.

"That's a threat, not a choice," Blade growled.

Hiss smiled, nodding his head toward the nearby woods. "Let's take a walk."

Blade clenched his fists. He didn't want to be distracted from his goal.

Then again, he was certain Hiss wasn't going to take no for an answer. The sooner they had their chat, the sooner he could return to more important matters.

"Let's get this over with," he muttered, stomping his way past the nearest line of trees.

Hiss was swiftly at his side, the musk of his cat filling the air.

"I thought your lack of social skills was because you were locked in a cage," he complained.

Blade sent his companion a warning glare. "Don't push me, Hiss. It's only because I owe you for getting me out of that cage that I haven't kicked your ass."

Hiss stiffened, an ancient pain darkening his eyes. "You don't owe me, Blade. Not ever."

Blade's guts twisted at the words, and he lost all bluster. No matter how much this Pantera male—or any of the Pantera, for that matter—pissed him off or pushed him too far, bottom line—they were family. Always there for one another. Ready to fight. Ready to draw blood.

Or spill it.

Stopping in the center of the small clearing, Blade turned to face the older male.

"Tell me what you want."

Hiss studied him for a long minute, as if searching for something in Blade's ever-guarded expression. Then, at last, he answered the question.

"Raphael's worried about you."

Blade's brows drew together. "Worried? Why?"

"You were expected to return to the Wildlands after you were freed from Benson's lab."

Blade's jaw tightened. He didn't do well with expectations. Not anymore. It'd been over two months, but there wasn't a night that went by he wasn't waking up covered in sweat, his brain still reeling from the nightmare that he was underground again, caged beneath the clinic in Baton Rouge.

"I did return," he said.

Hiss snorted. "For two nights."

Blade shrugged. He'd gone home to heal. His puma had needed to be surrounded by the magic of the Wildlands, where he could shift and run free. But it was a process that took less time for him than for most Pantera, since his role as Diplomat meant he spent long periods traveling around the world. His cat was used to being away and without its spiritual fuel, so to speak.

"Unlike the hell I came from, the Wildlands aren't a prison," he groused. "I'm free to come and go as I please."

Hiss scowled. "Of course you are, but you also have a duty to your people."

The words scraped against Blade's raw nerves. He was trying not to think about his duty. Or how he was turning his back on his kind when they needed him the most. Screw Hiss for reminding him, digging at him.

"I don't think you're in a position to talk about duty to your people," he snapped, only to instantly wince in regret. Hiss had spent years working with the enemy, been labeled a traitor—but he'd paid for his sins. Hardcore. And if the guilt that flared through the male's eyes now was any indication, he was still paying. "Shit, I'm sorry," Blade rasped.

And he was. Not only because Hiss had been the one to finally free him from that lab of horror, but because Blade was in no position to judge anyone.

"You're right," Hiss breathed, his voice harsh with pain. "I'm trying like hell to repair a portion of the damage that I caused, but I will never be able to fully pay for my sins."

Blade curled his hands, fighting the guilt of his own assholery while the anxious need to return to his hunt hummed powerfully through his body.

Christ, he felt like a string that had been pulled to the point of snapping.

His eyes flickered past Hiss to a pair of rabbits. Ears up, alert, they stared at him for a moment, then took off into the woods. "That's what I'm doing," he uttered.

"What?" Hiss asked.

His gaze returned to the Suit. "Dealing with the sins of the past."

Hiss studied him in confusion. Around them the breeze rustled through the boughs of the pine trees, scenting the air with a potent tang. A bird trilled a high-pitched song just above Blade's head, perhaps calling for a mate.

"Talk to me, Blade," Hiss urged.

Blade hesitated. Despite the nightmares, the cold sweat, the rage in his heart, he'd refused to discuss his time in Benson's lab. It was almost as if he feared that giving words to the horror he'd endured and seen would somehow grant it power over his life.

But he didn't have to explain to Hiss.

The male understood.

Granted, he'd been there only a short time. But that's all it took, really.

Blade cleared his throat and forced himself to speak.

"You know Benson was attempting to create some sort of super solider using our blood."

"Yeah." Hiss's features hardened with fury. "Goddess only knows how many Pantera and humans he killed in his Frankenstein labs."

The Pantera had been so distracted by the erosion of the Wildlands over the past fifty years they'd failed to realize that the true danger came from the humans.

In particular Christopher Benson, a madman who had been using Pantera blood to build his empire. Not to mention keeping himself alive well past his expiration date.

"That's not the only way he tried to create his soldiers," Blade said.

Hiss nodded. "So we discovered. We have several Pantera females who were forcibly impregnated with human semen."

"And human females impregnated with our semen," Blade added.

"True." Hiss jerked, as if he'd just been hit with an unseen blow. "Oh, shit. You're talking about what happened to you."

Blade gave a stiff nod. "Yes."

Hiss cleared his throat, trying to disguise his discomfort.

Blade's lips twisted. Yeah. There weren't many things more uncomfortable than two dudes talking about bodily fluids and having them forcibly removed from their private parts.

"Look, what happened in those labs wasn't your fault, Blade," Hiss at last said. "You were a victim."

Blade's teeth clenched. He refused to think of himself as a victim. It was too passive. He was a survivor.

And now, a Hunter.

"It doesn't matter who was to blame," Blade told his companion. "The only thing I care about is my young."

Hiss looked instantly confused, as if he was having major trouble processing what Blade had just said.

Blade could sympathize. It'd been weeks since he'd learned about the female carrying his child and he was still trying to digest the stunning information.

"You have a cub?" Hiss pressed.

The word fisted around Blade's heart. Always did. It was a terrifying and wonderful kind of magic. "There was a female who was impregnated with my seed."

"What? Are you sure?" Hiss held up his hand in an apologetic motion. No doubt he could sense that Blade's cat was pressing close to the surface. He might not be able to shift outside the Wildlands, but that didn't mean he couldn't do some serious damage if he snapped. "Sorry. I mean, we scoured through every medical file we could get our hands on and they showed a very low percentage of females who actually became pregnant."

Blade shuddered. If he closed his eyes he could still feel the crack of his bones as the guards beat him with their beloved metal baseball bats. True, they'd known they couldn't kill him, but they took perverse pleasure in making him suffer for his disobedience.

"Yeah, they weren't slow to express their frustration with the whole breeding program," he rasped.

Hiss tilted his head to the side, his puma visible in his eyes. "I never asked, and if you don't want to go there again I get it, but—"

"What did they do to me? What did they *want* from me?" Blade growled softly. "How did they go about getting it?"

Hiss remained silent, but his jaw tightened.

"I don't mind talking about it. Every Pantera should know their enemy and what it's capable of." He inhaled sharply and looked up at the trees, swaying in the breeze. "When they first captured me they spent most of their time just trying to keep me contained. I was…" A grim smile curved his lips. "Uncooperative."

Hiss snorted darkly. "I can imagine."

Not many things pleased Blade, but he took fierce pleasure in the knowledge that he'd managed to kill at least two of the guards and severely disabled a half dozen more. He'd also destroyed everything in the lab, ripped the bars off all the windows, and made his Pantera battle cry heard to the rest of the prisoners on the floor before they'd managed to force his ass in that cage.

"There's always payback, of course. They drugged me with malachite to the point where I could barely function. Just breathing was a fucking chore." Malachite was the one certain way to weaken a Pantera. It was their kryptonite. And with males like Blade, the guards liked to double, even triple the dosage. "I'm not sure how long I was there. Maybe a few weeks, maybe months; the days all blended together. But eventually they discovered the perfect amount of malachite to use on me—to control me—to force the seed from my cock."

A dark, fierce growl rumbled in Hiss's chest, the air heating with the power of his cat. "They don't deserve to continue breathing."

"Many of them don't breathe. Not anymore, thank the Goddess."

"It's still not enough."

"No. It's not." Blade struggled to contain the fury that pooled like lava in the depths of his being. He feared that one day he would explode and all the anger and bitterness housed within him would spew to the surface and he would have no control, no reason. These days, he truly did everything he could to keep his emotions tightly leashed.

It was the only way to remain focused on his goal.

"I don't know why," he continued coldly. "Maybe they believed human females needed a male close, needed our musk to become fertile, but they put me in the same room with this one for her procedure." He flared his nose. "I had to watch as they used tools to impregnate her. I had to watch as she struggled against the drugs they gave her to keep her compliant, my body unable to move, to fight."

Hiss sucked in a deep breath, making a visible effort to regain command of his inner beast. It wasn't easy. For a Pantera male not to be able to care for a female, fight for her, protect her… There was nothing worse.

Except perhaps if that human female carried a cub, Blade thought darkly, and there were two out there in the world he couldn't get to, couldn't protect.

"And they call *us* animals," Hiss growled.

"Now you see…understand…what I'm doing here. Why…"

"Yes. But, brother, even if you were in the same room with her, you can't know if the procedure worked. Our noses are sharp, but they can't detect anything that early."

"I remember her scent," Blade said succinctly, refusing to add that the soft floral smell of her caramel skin was forever emblazoned on his soul, along with the vision of her perfect oval face, which was framed by long, sable hair and golden eyes. Eyes that had been both fierce and fearful as they'd tried to focus during the procedure. "And when you returned to free us, my cat picked up that scent once again. Along with a new one. One she carried with her."

Hiss seemed to know instinctively what Blade was talking about. "She was pregnant," he uttered.

Blade's heart gave that same aching twist whenever he tried to imagine his child growing in the female's womb.

A cub...

His cub.

"Yes."

Hiss reached out to squeeze Blade's shoulder. "Why didn't you bring her to the Wildlands?"

"I lost her. She disappeared during the battle against Benson's guards." He made a low sound of frustration. His first instinct had been to follow her. Screw everything but his overriding need to protect his young. But the sounds of his brothers and sisters in battle as they fought to rescue those still in cages had lured him away. "I tried to track her down, but my instinct, my skills were too weak. I was forced to return home and heal my cat. But once I was strong enough, I resumed my hunt."

Hiss frowned. "You could have gone to Raph and told him what had happened. He would have understood your need. Hell, he would have sent a dozen Hunters to help with your search."

Blade gave a sharp shake of his head. "That's exactly why I didn't say anything. I have to do this alone."

"I used to believe that too, but I was wrong, my brother." Hiss gave Blade's shoulder another squeeze. "We need each other. Now more than ever."

"Not with this."

"We're family."

Blade held up a silencing hand. "No." His voice was hard. Unrelenting. "You don't get what they did to this woman. She was tied to a gurney, drugged, her legs forced apart, terrified out of her mind while they forcibly inseminated her."

"Shit."

Blade's lips twisted at Hiss's horrified expression. "Yeah. If I come charging in with a dozen Pantera, at best she's going to freak the fuck out, try to run. At worst, she could try to fight and get herself and our cub hurt."

Hiss offered a grudging nod of agreement as the wind around them picked up and sent the trees listing sideways. "How do you intend to find her?"

"I went to Baton Rouge first, but they'd already torched the clinic."

"They're growing annoyingly predictable."

The Pantera had discovered that Christopher Benson had a habit of covering his tracks by immediately setting any evidence of his terror on fire. He'd burned at least a dozen properties in the past few months.

"I did, however, manage to track down one of the lab techs who was stupid enough to remain in town," Blade said.

Hiss arched a brow. "Did he talk?"

Blade snorted. The human male had startled babbling the second Blade kicked in his door. *No honor among thieves* was the philosophy of Benson's goons.

"He did better," Blade told his companion. "He had a laptop he'd stolen from the clinic before it was destroyed, no doubt hoping to cash in somehow."

Hiss stepped forward, anticipation sizzling in the air. "You have files from Benson?"

Blade grimaced. He'd been as excited as Hiss when the human had tossed the laptop at him before jumping out the window in a futile attempt to escape justice. It'd taken less than ten minutes to discover that his excitement had been premature.

"Most of the files had been corrupted," he admitted. "I'm assuming that someone triggered a virus to wipe out the information."

Hiss growled. "Of course they did. Fuck!"

Blade released a short, humorless laugh. Nothing had been simple when trying to track down and destroy Christopher Benson.

"But I did recover a file that contained a list of the human patients who were admitted to the clinic over the past year," he said.

"Did you find your female on the list?"

"I'm still not sure."

"Why not?"

"Because I never heard her name."

"Oh, hell." Hiss grimaced, no doubt recalling the fact that they'd all been identified with a combination of numbers and letters. Like they were fucking lab specimens.

"How many names on the list?" Hiss asked.

"Thirty females."

"And you're tracking down each one?"

Blade nodded. The list had only given names and addresses. There were no ages or identifying descriptions that might have allowed him to narrow down the search.

"I've already found twenty of them."

"Ten to go," Hiss murmured, his expression revealing he was struggling against his instinctive urge to offer his help.

Pantera possessed a primitive need to protect. Especially each other. On any other day, with any other situation, Blade would've been grateful for the help.

But this...her...

"I'm getting closer," Blade muttered, his attention suddenly distracted as the breeze once again changed direction.

There was something in the air. Something familiar. Something...floral.

"And when you find her?" Hiss asked.

Blade was already turning away, his senses on full alert. "I'm claiming my cub."

Chapter 2

The café at the end of Main Street looked like something out of a classic TV show. Black and white tiled floor, with a long counter and stools that had seats covered with red vinyl. A small eating area with booths that was next to a long front window, and a half-wall that divided the café and the kitchen, allowing the owner and cook, Fran Meyer, to keep an eye on her customers.

Nearing her fortieth birthday, Fran kept her long hair dyed a bright red and her lips a glossy pale pink. Granted, no one referred to her as pretty with her short, square frame, hooked nose, and small eyes, but she was kind as well as brisk and efficient. And she always had a smile for her customers.

The young waitress Valli Landry, on the other hand, was young and beautiful, with her dark hair pulled into a thick braid that fell down her back and wide, golden eyes. She was taller than most women in the small town of Bonne, and reed slender, although it was hard to tell with the smock top she'd started to wear with a pair of stretchy yoga pants.

She'd explained her fashion choice to Fran by claiming that the lifesaving treatments she'd received during her time in the Baton Rouge clinic had left her skin too sensitive for the traditional uniform she used to wear.

She wasn't prepared to tell anyone the truth. Hell, she barely wanted to claim it herself.

Massaging her lower back, Valli glanced around the empty dining room. It was that quiet time between the lunch and dinner crowd, which meant that it was a perfect opportunity to wipe down the tables, mop the floor, and replenish the glass case that they kept filled with Fran's amazingly delicious cakes, pies, and muffins.

Grabbing the mop, she got to it. Work like this, mindless yet physical, was her utter salvation. With each swish of the cotton ropes, each wring-out of the rag, from dirty to clean, she felt as though her recent past was far away. And at times, that it no longer existed. That she was still the carefree, innocent young woman she'd been before.

But the feeling didn't last long. Never did.

She needed to get the pastries, fill the case, and then maybe she could take that long overdue break she and her sore feet had been craving for the past hour.

Walking around the edge of the counter, she entered the kitchen and headed toward the walk-in refrigerator. Instantly, Fran stopped peeling the large mound of potatoes she had soaking in the sink and glanced over her shoulder.

"Where do you think you're going?" the older woman demanded.

Valli looked at her in surprise. "The pies are almost gone. I was going to cut one of the apple and maybe a coconut cream."

Fran wiped her hands on a towel as she moved toward Valli. "I'll take care of that. You eat your dinner."

"It's okay, I'm not really hungry," Valli forced herself to say, only to grimace when her stomach loudly grumbled.

Fran chuckled. "You can't fool me, girl." Reaching for Valli, she took her arm and firmly guided her toward the small table at the back of the kitchen, where a hot roast beef sandwich and a large pile of French fries was waiting for her. This time, Valli's stomach rumbled appreciatively at the scent that wafted toward her.

Ever since her return to Bonne, she'd craved meat with an urgency that was terrifying. And to think, just last year she'd started thinking seriously about becoming vegan.

Dropping into the wood chair with the soft red cushion, Valli gave in to the inevitable. Not only would Fran continue to hover over her until she cleaned her plate, but her feet really did hurt and she was feeling a little dizzy. Maybe eating something substantial would help clear her head.

"I want you to finish every bit of that," Fran warned, scurrying around the kitchen to collect a glass of milk and one of Valli's favorite pralines.

"You don't have to fuss over me," Valli protested.

Fran smiled. "I like fussing over you."

A warm sensation moved through Valli, and while taking a ravenous bite of her sandwich, she ruefully acknowledged that her employer was far closer to a mother figure than her own.

Of course, that wasn't saying much.

Valli's mother had been an alcoholic who'd lived with an endless series of disgusting and despicable men. Which had, of course, forced Valli to live with them too. By the time she'd turned sixteen, she'd had enough of fighting off those piece-of-shit perverts and hit the road. She doubted her mother even knew she was gone.

For seven years she'd traveled from one town to another, working at restaurants and truck stops, until she'd met Fran on a bus as she was going from Shreveport to New Orleans.

The older woman had seemed to sense that Valli was alone in the world and simply drifting from place to place. She'd offered her a job as a waitress, along with the use of a small apartment above the restaurant.

Valli had agreed, but she'd been prepared to discover that the offer was some sort of con. In her experience, people didn't do things out of the kindness of their heart.

There was always a cost.

But as the days, and then weeks, coasted past, she'd slowly settled into the quiet life of Bonne and the comfort of Fran's soft heart. Granted, she didn't want to be a waitress in a backwater town forever, but it was nice to know she had a peaceful place to stay and a way to earn a decent living until she decided what she wanted from her future.

Then, without warning, she'd been hit with a strange illness. It'd started with just a basic cold, but one she couldn't seem to shake. After a week and a half, she'd gone to the local doctor, who'd given her a home remedy that he swore was better than any antibiotics.

But it hadn't been.

She'd grown sicker and sicker, getting to the point where she could barely crawl out of bed. She wasn't working, and poor Fran had to hire on another waitress. As the guilt and worry built inside of her, the doctor performed endless tests trying to figure out what was wrong. In the end, he'd had to concede defeat.

He couldn't heal her, but he knew of a clinic in Baton Rouge…

She often wondered, when she was in that cell, what the doctor had or hadn't known.

With a small shake of her head, Valli pulled herself out of her dark thoughts and forced a smile to her lips.

"I don't know what I would do without you, Fran," she said with a soft sincerity.

"Nonsense." The older woman flushed with pleasure even as she tried to wave away Valli's gratitude. "Eat up and then take a walk. The dinner crowd won't be coming in for another hour."

Waiting for Fran to return to her potato peeling, Valli bent over her plate and finished the meal with a gluttony that she couldn't control. For the past two months she'd been eating like a horse and could never fully satisfy the gnawing hunger deep inside her.

Barely resisting the urge to lick her empty plate, she forced herself to her feet. Instantly, the dizziness returned with a vengeance. Damn.

Walking out of the kitchen with careful steps, Valli wondered if Fran suspected she wasn't feeling well. Again. If so, the older woman would insist that she go upstairs to bed. It was such a temptation, but it would not only leave Fran alone to deal with both cooking and waiting tables—it would be a reminder of the last time she'd been unwell. And she couldn't risk losing her job, even if Fran let her stay upstairs while she hired out again. She had to push through.

Once out of the kitchen, she scurried down the short hallway that led to the women's bathroom. Crossing to the sink, she splashed cold water on her face, taking deep breaths.

After a moment or two the dizziness receded but was replaced by a strange sense of euphoria. As if something, or someone, was filling her with pure joy.

Unnerved by the sensation, Valli rushed out of the bathroom, only to slam into a man who was just entering the hallway.

Dr. Scott Richards reached out to grasp her by the shoulders, preventing her from bouncing away like a pinball.

"Valli, are you okay?" he asked in concern.

She instantly pulled away from his touch. It wasn't personal. The doctor was young and boy-next-door handsome, with his dark blond hair and bright blue eyes. He even had dimples. But since her return from the clinic she didn't want anyone touching her. Especially not men.

She forced a smile to her lips. "Sorry, Dr. Richards."

He clicked his tongue. "How many times do I need to tell you to call me Scott? Dr. Richards was my dad."

She took another step backward. Since her arrival in Bonne, she sensed that Scott wanted more from her than just a doctor/patient relationship.

"Scott," she reluctantly offered.

"That's better." He flashed his dimples. "Now why don't you join me for a cup of coffee? You look like you could use some caffeine."

"I'm fine."

He frowned. "You're pale."

"I'm working a double shift, so it's been a long day."

"Hmm." His gaze studied the shadows she knew marred the skin beneath her eyes before lowering to her loose smock. Did he suspect there was something she was trying to hide? Or was he just surprised in her choice of uniform? "I think you need to come in for a checkup."

A flush of anxiety moved through Valli at his words. She pressed herself against the wall and began to inch her way toward the back door that served as an emergency exit.

She liked this man. She really did. But there was no way in hell she was allowing him to examine her. No way in hell she was letting him even get close enough to try.

"I told you when I returned to town that I was cured."

The blue gaze moved over her face. "So you said, but you haven't really told me what the treatments involved and if you need any follow-up care."

"I don't need anything," she pressed a little breathlessly. "It's over. I'm fine."

He looked unconvinced. She didn't blame him. "I'd like to run a few tests to satisfy myself that you're healthy."

Her head was feeling extraordinarily heavy and her hands were tingling. She prayed it was just anxiety. She moved another few inches toward the door. She needed fresh air. And space to breathe.

"I'll call and make an appointment later," she lied.

But Scott wasn't fooled. He folded his arms over his chest, sending her a stern frown.

"I have time tomorrow morning."

She shook her head. "I'm working."

"Come on now, Fran isn't a slave driver," he said, clearly aware that the older woman treated Valli like a long-lost daughter. "I'm sure she would give you an hour off."

Another inch, and another. Her mouth was so dry. She'd reached the doorjamb.

"I can't."

Scott heaved a frustrated sigh. "I'm worried about you, Valli."

"I told you," she said through slightly gritted teeth. "I'm fine."

"Prove it. Come in and let me do a few tests." He stepped toward her, reaching out his hand as if he intended to touch her face.

"No!" Valli leaped to the side, like a cat who'd just been burned.

Scott froze, his expression hardening at her melodramatic response. "I'm sorry."

Her heart slamming against her ribs, Valli grabbed the doorknob and turned. "I really am okay."

He didn't believe a word she was saying, and no doubt was thinking she might have an emotional or mental issue to deal with now. "At least promise me you'll call if you need anything, even if it's just a friendly shoulder to lean on."

"I promise," she lied again, this time forcing a stiff smile.

Then, unable to halt her overwhelming need to get away, she shoved open the door and darted outside.

Distantly she was aware of Scott calling out her name and the crunch of gravel beneath her feet as she scurried toward the nearby woods. Oh God, yes… Air. Light...

She knew she was acting crazy. A grown woman didn't have to run away from a doctor who was only trying to help her.

But she couldn't help it. Something was…ruling her. Something she didn't understand. Ever since she'd returned, it was as if her body was no longer her own.

Like she couldn't control her impulses.

Preoccupied with that unnerving thought, she didn't hear the sound of approaching footsteps until they were nearly upon her. Shit! *The doctor?* Her blood went cold in her veins and she reacted on pure instinct. Spinning around, she used her momentum to put power behind her fist as she directed it straight at the chin of the man standing behind her.

Valli had learned to fight at a young age. It was the only way to survive in a house filled with a steady stream of predatory pieces of shit. But even she was surprised by the loud crack as her knuckles connected with the stranger's jaw.

He stumbled backward from the impact, but as she turned to scamper back to the safety of the diner, he was already reaching out to grab her hand.

"Easy," he murmured, his expression rueful as he reached up to rub his chin. "That's a hell of a right hook you have."

Shock jolted through her as she caught the rich musk that teased at her nose.

Oh, fuck.

Oh, no.

Her entire body went rigid. Her breath locked inside her lungs as she tilted back her head to see the man's face.

Horror consumed her entire being and she froze in place, like a terrified rabbit. The man who towered above her had dark, smoldering eyes and golden hair that shimmered in the stray sunlight that peeked through the trees. He was chillingly good looking, with a full mouth and lean, compelling features that had haunted her dreams for the past two months.

"It's you," she breathed in alarm.

His expression was unreadable. "You remember me?"

Shaking now, her sharp laugh echoed eerily through the woodland. "It's hard to forget the animal who raped me."

He sucked in a harsh breath and his eyes went wide with shock, as if he was utterly appalled at her accusation.

"Raped," he rasped, dropping her hand as if she'd burned him. "What the hell?"

She glared up at him. Strangely, now that she recognized him, had confronted him, her terror shifted into something akin to fury, outrage. She didn't want to run from him; she wanted to punch him again. Knock that fake look of shock off his face.

"I know it was you." She spat out the words, a bitter need to not just physically hurt this man but emotionally hurt him as well churning through her. "I see your face every time I close my eyes."

He shook his head. "I don't understand. I was at the clinic, just like you. I was a prisoner, just like you."

That fury and outrage bubbled inside of her now, hot and deadly. How dare he claim he was some sort of victim? How dare he say he was anything like her?

"You're an animal," she ground out.

His jaw clenched at that. "I'm a Pantera."

"I know what you're capable of. You can shift into a cat."

"A puma, yes," he agreed, his voice edged with a fierce pride.

Clearly he wasn't going to admit what he'd done. Not even attempt to atone for his savage actions. Pig! She knew she should run, get the hell away from him. He wasn't here to talk, she was sure of that. But several things besides nightmares had come out of her experience in the clinic. She'd grown a pair. And they were huge and made of metal. If cornered now, she wouldn't give in without one helluva fight.

"Maybe I'll just refresh your memory," she continued harshly through gritted teeth. "And bear in mind, there are people who care about me within shouting distance, so I advise you to remain where you are." Her eyes bored into his. "You were at the clinic to sell your blood—"

"What?" Confusion rippled over his severely handsome face as he interrupted her. "There's no way I would sell my blood. Ever." A growl escaped his throat. "I was captured by Benson's assholes and kept caged in the basement of the clinic."

Valli hesitated, her brows drawing together. A shard of interest, of curiosity, pricked at her. Could he be... No! She shoved the thoughts away. Of course, he would try to deny his sins. No man would be willing to admit he'd forced himself on a woman.

"Liar," she rasped.

His eyes went clear then, and his chin lifted. "I don't lie. That's a human trait."

The harsh, deep sincerity threading his voice made her stomach clench with a strange unease.

She shook her head. "They told me everything," she said. "What you did...what you—"

"Who?" he demanded. "Who told you?"

"The doctors."

A low snarl rumbled in his throat, his eyes smoldering with a lethal power. "They're the liars."

She licked her dry lips. "Right."

He leaned down until their noses were nearly touching. Valli inhaled sharply but didn't move away. *Stupid! Stupid fool! Why are you still standing here? Letting him breathe your air?*

His eyes closed then, and he just held steady, as if he was mentally willing her to believe his words.

"I'm telling you the truth," he whispered. "They lied to all of us. Manipulated all of us. *Hurt* all of us."

Heat poured into her and she nearly lost her footing. Over the past two months, she had considered exactly what she would do if she ever found this man. At the top of that list had been slicing open his chest and yanking out his heart. She'd assumed that would kill even a Pantera.

But the last thing she'd ever expected to do was to allow him to be this close to her as they debated his guilt.

Fool!

"Don't touch me," she snapped, ripping away from his strange, almost warm, connection. "Ever again."

His eyes snapped open. They were dark and deep and they implored her. "I would never hurt you."

Her lip curled. Was he serious? "You've already ruined my life."

In seconds, those deep, soulful eyes and potently male features hardened like granite. Not with the strain of a guilty conscience as she'd hoped, but with regret.

Maybe even pity.

He stepped back, moving away from her, and leaned against a massive cypress. He crossed his arms over his chest.

"What exactly did the doctors tell you?"

Breathless and frustratingly confused, she warned herself not to answer. She'd gone from naïve to stupid in minutes here. She should be hauling ass back to the diner, to safety. Or kicking the lethal shifter standing before her in the nuts.

Instead, she found the words tumbling from her foolish lips.

"They said that the only way to cure my illness was with a special serum."

His brows knit together. "Serum? You mean Pantera blood?" he demanded.

"I didn't know it was that. Not at first." Distaste curled her lips. "But then they said I would die unless I agreed to have a transfusion."

Without warning, a blast of heat filled the air between them. She knew at once it was coming from the man. And he hadn't even moved.

"You call me an animal but you were quick enough to accept my blood," he accused in harsh tones.

Valli flinched. Not out of fear this time, but from something else.

She searched for the answer and came up with guilt. *No.* She wouldn't allow that. Yes, admittedly, she had accepted that serum, even knowing what it was. But she'd believed it had been given willingly.

Her throat tightened. And if it hadn't been given willingly...

Her eyes lifted to meet his. She swallowed. What choice had there been? Live or die. That's what the doctors had told her.

"It was the only way," she said softly, almost pained.

The male sucked in a deep breath as overhead clouds enveloped the sun.

"It cured you?" he asked, as if it was an effort to speak calmly.

"I felt better, yes. But they insisted on bringing me back to the lab for more tests, and that's when you—"

Her words broke off as the memory flashed through her mind. It came in odd bursts, like a strobe light flashing images that were there and gone so fast she couldn't hold on to them. The only thing she remembered with any clarity was this man's starkly handsome face.

And the pain.

Without warning, a rush of dizziness assaulted her. The worst she'd ever felt. She gasped and reached for something, anything, as black flecks danced before her eyes and her stomach heaved.

The man was beside her in an instant, grasping her shoulders, supporting her.

"Know this, female. I did nothing," he growled, so close that she could feel the heat of the body through her clothing. "I swear on my Goddess."

Nauseous and so weak, Valli reached up to wipe the sweat from her brow. What was wrong? What was happening? Was it the changes in her body making her sick? Or God... no, was her previous illness returning?

"I saw you," she said, desperate to hide her growing weakness.

"You saw my face," he corrected.

She groaned, the dizziness making it difficult to think clearly.

"Do you actually remember me..." he began, struggling with the words. "...fucking hell... Do you remember me hurting you?"

She flinched. *No.* "It's because... I've blocked it out." *Must have. Must have...*

"You don't remember it," he insisted, his voice hard. "Because it never happened."

She gave another jerk of her arm. This time she managed to free herself.

"It happened," she insisted.

"How can you be so sure?"

Her face jerked up, her blurry vision receding enough so she could see him clearly for a moment. "Because I'm pregnant!"

She expected shock in those dark depths. Horror. Maybe even violence.

Instead his male features softened as he reached out to lay a gentle hand against the swell of her belly hidden beneath the smock top.

"I know," he breathed in genuine awe. "You carry my cub. *Our* cub."

Her breath suddenly felt as if it were being wrenched from her lungs, and the ground tilted beneath her feet. But it wasn't until she was falling face first toward the ground that she realized she was fainting. Distantly, she heard the sound of the doctor calling her name over and over.

"Valli! Valli, where are you?"

She couldn't answer. Instead, she felt herself being scooped into a pair of strong arms.

Shit.

Chapter 3

The Wildlands, deep in the bayous of Louisiana, were shrouded in mystery. The private and ancient land of the Pantera was well protected to keep out their enemies, and the new flood of curiosity-seekers.

Behind the magical barriers, the Pantera lived in simple houses and cabins that were built in harmony with the lush vegetation and towering cypress trees. But they weren't complete savages.

At the very heart of the Wildlands, a new Headquarters was being completed that housed the Geeks and their Pentagon-grade computer system. Plus, the Nurturers had built one of the world's finest medical facilities.

Not that it looked like a traditional hospital. There was no smell of antiseptic or disinfectant. There were no florescent lights, and the architecture and design was anything but cold and sterile. Instead, the morning sun shone through the open windows and the air was laced with healing plants and the gentle musk of Pantera.

The room where Blade had been restlessly pacing all night had cherry-paneled walls, handwoven rugs on the wooden floor, and large windows to overlook the communal eating space.

Across the room was a wide bed where Valli was lying unconscious, a soft blue blanket covering her legs and a fluffy pillow under her head. Leaning over her, Jean-Baptiste was completing his examination.

The male looked more like a biker than one of their best Healers. He was over six feet, with a broad chest and lean muscle beneath his jeans and casual tee. His hair was dark brown and fell past his jawline, while his eyes flashed with amber fire. And as he straightened, the overhead light revealed the numerous tattoos that created a dazzling display of art on his skin.

Blade continued to pace as the Healer left the bed and walked across the room to speak with him.

It'd been sheer impulse to bring Valli to the Wildlands after she'd fainted. There no doubt had been a doctor in her local town. And certainly there were hospitals in Baton Rouge and New Orleans.

But Blade hadn't even considered taking her to any of them.

Instead, he'd scooped her up in his arms and run directly to this facility.

Home.

There was no way in hell he was trusting anyone but Pantera to offer medical care to this female.

Jean-Baptiste held up a hand. "You're going to wear a hole in the floor, *mon ami.*"

Blade forced himself to come to a halt, despite the anxiety that continued to hum through his body.

He would never forget holding Valli's limp body in his arms as he'd run, focused and furiously, through the fields and swamps. It was the first time he'd ever truly touched her, held her, and she'd felt so unbearably fragile. So vulnerable.

"How is she?" he demanded. "She's been out all night."

"She's well, and starting to come around."

Relief coursed through him. "And the cub?"

"Healthy."

"Thank the Goddess," he breathed, his jaw so tight it pained him. As he'd run with Valli in his arms, he'd been able to sense the cub's heartbeats. They'd amazingly seemed to sync with his own, almost as if the two of them were already bonded. Still, he needed Jean-Baptiste's reassurance. "Why did she faint?"

The large male folded his arms over his chest. "It's not uncommon for pregnant women to have fainting spells from time to time. But for her, my guess is that it was more psychological stress than any physical problem. Though clearly she was also exhausted."

Guilt blasted through Blade. Stress. Shit. That was his fault. He'd been so intent on tracking down the female who carried his child that he'd never considered her reaction to his abrupt appearance.

"I should have taken more care not to frighten her," he rasped.

"But I had no idea that..."

Jean-Baptiste frowned. "No idea about what?"

His eyes met and held the Healer's. "She believes I raped her, Baptiste."

A thick silence filled the room as his Pantera brother stared at him in shocked disbelief. Finally, after a few moments, the male gave a sharp shake of his head.

"No way."

Blade clenched his hands. Just the accusation of hurting a woman made his gut twist with revulsion.

"They lied to her, of course. She was drugged during the procedure and only has fractured memories of what happened," he explained. "I was in the room with her, and I remember her looking at me, her eyes glassy, pained. She didn't know where she was. And I fucking couldn't help her..." A growl escaped his throat. "Afterward, the doctors must've convinced her that she was attacked by a Pantera."

"Attacked by you," Baptiste clarified with a snarl. "Just when I think those bastards can't get any more evil, they manage to prove me wrong."

Blade didn't want to think about Benson or his associates. He was worried his cat would emerge and go on a hunt for flesh and blood. A hunt that would keep him away from Valli and their cub. Right now, he needed to be fully focused on the woman he'd been hunting for the past two months.

"I was trying to assure her that I would never hurt her when she passed out," he told his companion.

"Hmm." Jean-Baptiste strolled back toward the bed, standing next to the mattress as he gazed down at Valli.

Blade went to the other side. As he gazed down at the beautiful female who had never left his thoughts for a moment since the clinic, his puma pressed against his skin with a fierce agitation.

Clearly, his beast was deeply disturbed by Valli's unnatural stillness. And equally disturbed to have another male hovering so close to her.

"What is it?" he demanded as the Healer continued to study her with intense concentration.

"I'm wondering if they did more than just give her drugs and impregnate her," the male said.

Blade frowned. "Talk to me, Jean-Baptiste."

The Healer lifted his head to meet Blade's worried gaze. "I sensed barriers in her mind when I was examining her."

"Barriers?"

Jean-Baptiste shrugged. "I wasn't sure what they were. Now I'm beginning to suspect the humans used hypnosis of some kind to block out her memories, or even plant new ones."

Blade was caught off guard. "Why?"

The Healer looked like he was considering the various possibilities before he finally answered.

"You said she originally went to the clinic because she was sick?"

Blade grimaced, recalling her words when she'd confessed she'd willingly accepted Pantera blood.

"She said that she was dying."

Jean-Baptiste nodded, apparently unconcerned that Valli had been gravely ill. Blade assumed that meant whatever had been killing her was now cured.

"Then presumably she wasn't expecting to become a mother," the male said.

Blade blinked. He hadn't considered the fact that, unlike many females who'd gone to Benson's clinics around the country, she hadn't been interested in conceiving a child.

"Shit," he cursed on a dark breath. "They needed an explanation of how she ended up pregnant."

Baptiste nodded. "Exactly."

It made sense. If the doctors had convinced Valli that she'd been raped, it would explain how she got pregnant, as well as encourage her to remain at the clinic so she could both stay protected and hide the fact that she was carrying the child of an animal.

Blade's jaw tightened as he was reminded of Valli's reaction when she'd recognized him.

Fear. Anger. Disgust.

"God. Damn."

He felt his cat begin to emerge, rage unleashing his beast.

Jean-Baptiste sent him a warning glance. "Easy, *mon ami*," he warned. "She's a victim."

Blade shoved the animal back with a grunt, then forced himself to take a deep, calming breath. Goddess, how could Baptiste even suggest it? He wasn't angry with Valli. He wanted to gut those bastards who'd done this to her. Who'd lied to her. Hurt her. Manipulated her. And ruined...fuck!...any hope for a relationship between them, not to mention possibly destroying her ability to love her own child.

The idea of that...well, it seared through his blood like acid.

"I think she's starting to wake," Jean-Baptiste said as Valli sighed softly. The Healer leaned forward and reached out to place his hand on her forehead.

Without warning, Blade's puma released a rumbling growl, his claws poking through the tips of his fingers.

"Don't," he snarled brutally. He didn't want the male touching her.

And, clearly, neither did his cat.

Jean-Baptiste froze, as if he realized that Blade could easily be provoked into an act of violence he would later regret. After all, the Healer had a female of his own that he was insanely protective of.

"I think I can help her to recover her true memories," Baptiste said in low, calm tones, his hands at his sides now. His eyes lifted to meet Blade's. "Do you want me to try, *mon ami?*"

With everything he had in him, Blade attempted to leash his primitive reaction. No matter how much the cat wanted out, fangs bared, he was far more concerned with Valli's health than with any male's need to possess her. And while he'd spent a vast majority of his life traveling in his role as a Diplomat, he was well aware that Jean-Baptiste was considered to have a magical touch, especially for those who suffered mental and emotional challenges.

He managed a jerky nod. "Yes."

Jean-Baptiste brushed his fingers gently over Valli's forehead. On cue, her lashes fluttered open.

Her golden eyes were dark with a sleepy confusion as she glanced up at the large man bent over her.

"Where am I?" she croaked.

"You're in the Wildlands," Jean-Baptiste told her in a gentle voice.

She blinked, as if struggling to accept his words. "What? How?"

Blade moved to perch on the edge of the mattress, careful not to crowd her. The last thing he wanted was to startle her into passing out again.

"I brought you here last night," he said.

Her head turned on the pillow, a subtle emotion rippling over her face. Relief? His heart raced at the thought she might be happy that he was near, only to skid to a halt when her eyes narrowed with accusation.

"You kidnapped me."

He clenched his teeth. And his heart squeezed with a pain he'd never felt before. No matter how hard it was, he couldn't take her suspicion personally, not when she'd been hypnotized into believing he was a savage animal.

"I brought you to the one place you could get the medical care you need," he assured her.

Her gaze moved to take in the hand-carved furniture and the pretty lace curtains. "It's not the one place," she said uneasily. "There's a doctor in my town—"

"A small-town doctor isn't what you need."

"I know what I need," she countered. "What is this place? It looks like a hotel."

"It's a hospital," Jean-Baptiste answered. "We prefer our patients to be as comfortable as possible."

She licked her lips, her hand unsteady as she lifted it to push back the hair that had escaped her tight braid. "I'm not your patient."

"Have you been fainting or feeling faint regularly?" the Healer asked, undeterred by her caustic response.

She didn't answer right away, which was probably an answer in itself.

"I need to get home, get back," she uttered breathlessly. "I have a job. My boss will be worried about me—"

"Please, calm down," Jean-Baptiste urged. "Right now your main concern should be yourself and your health." His fingers lingered on Valli's forehead. Blade suspected that he was using his powers to soothe her fears. "Physically, there's nothing wrong with you."

Sudden terror flared in her expression. "Oh my God, my baby?"

"Perfectly healthy," Jean-Baptiste confirmed.

Blade didn't miss her shudder of relief, the quick glimmer of tears in her eyes. Warmth filled his heart, and a rush of gratitude. Whatever her confused and angry feelings toward him, it was obvious she cared deeply about their child.

"Then why am I here?" she demanded, trying to sit up.

The Healer placed another pillow under her head so she could be slightly upright. "Blade was concerned when you fainted."

"Blade?" She whirled back to study Blade with a skittish gaze.

"That's your name?"

His lips twisted into a humorless smile. "A little late for introductions, I know, but yes." He nodded toward the male across the bed. "And that's Jean-Baptiste. A Pantera healer. One of our best."

She frowned. "I don't get this. I thought there was nothing wrong with me. Why would I need a healer?"

"I said nothing was physically wrong," Jean-Baptiste clarified.

Her stunningly beautiful face tightened, as if she was offended by the words, her hand reaching up to brush away Jean-Baptiste's hand.

"I'm not crazy," she ground out.

"No one said you were," Blade said, reaching to grasp her hand, which lay on top of the light blanket covering her body. Thankfully she made no effort to pull away from his grasp this time.

He hated it, but he needed to touch her.

To feel the heat of her skin and hear the steady beat of her heart.

"Then what are you saying?" she demanded, once again turning her attention to the Healer.

Jean-Baptiste chose his words with care. "I suspect that the doctors at the clinic used hypnosis to distort your memories."

Valli flinched, her fear scenting the air. Blade's cat pressed beneath his skin, wanting out. It didn't understand human deceit or betrayal. It only knew that this female was afraid and in need of comfort.

"No," she breathed. "You're just trying to protect your friend after what he..." She didn't finish.

This time it was Blade who pulled his hand from hers.

With a growl.

Jean-Baptiste's amber eyes glowed with outrage as he locked eyes with Valli. "Blade is one of my brothers, but if he ever harmed a vulnerable woman I would make him sorry he was born."

"Yes, he would." Blade confirmed. He knew exactly what Jean-Baptiste would do to him. "The male is an artist with a scalpel."

She said nothing to that, but at least the fear seeped from her gaze somewhat. The poor female, Blade thought. She was confused, not knowing who to trust, what to believe.

"Will you allow me to try and get rid of the barriers they placed in your mind?" Jean-Baptiste asked her gently.

"What?" She sat up completely now and moved back until she was pressed against the headboard. Her expression was wary, although the acrid scent of fear had defused to a tang of uncertainty. "I don't get any of this. I need to go home."

"I just want to give you the option of seeing the truth of what happened for yourself," Jean-Baptiste continued, his simple words as compelling as any flowery speech.

Valli bit her bottom lip, her eyes troubled. Was she wavering between her distrust of the Pantera and a new and sudden uncertainty in her own memories?

"Please," Blade added.

She glanced up at the door. "Do I have a choice?"

Jean-Baptiste scowled. "Of course you do."

"You're our guest, Valli," Blade said. "Not our prisoner. Walk out right now if you want to. I swear to the Goddess we are only trying to help you."

Sudden tears sprang to her eyes and she shook her head. "This is so unfair. I don't know who to trust anymore. What to believe."

Blade glanced over at the Healer. "Jean-Baptiste. We need a minute. Alone."

Baptiste raised his brow, then turned to his patient. "What do you say to that?"

Valli looked surprised that her needs would even be considered. "Me?"

He nodded. "Of course. As your Healer, my loyalty is to you."

Chapter 4

Loyalty. Healer.

Shifter. Wildlands.

Lies. Truth.

The words swam inside of Valli's head as the door closed behind Jean-Baptiste. The afternoon sun shone through the window at her back, illuminating one long strip of blue blanket.

Illuminating her right hand and Blade's left. He'd pulled it from her once, but it had found its way back. And she was...strangely glad.

She stared at the two. One, pale and feminine with unpolished nails. And the other, large and rough, with thick fingers which, if called upon, could turn into claws.

Her heart sped up inside her chest.

She was in the Wildlands, a place she'd only ever heard of. A place that after she'd left the clinic, after she'd found out what had happened to her, only brought on nightmares. But had those things happened to her? Or was what the Healer had said true? Had the doctors abducted her mind, her memories?

She'd never felt exactly comfortable with the doctors at the clinic, true. Hell, she hadn't felt comfortable taking blood from another either. But she'd been desperate.

And desperation had the ability to make one blind, deaf, and reckless.

Her eyes slowly lifted to meet the concerned black ones of the male she'd been told had assaulted her. It was strange. Her mind suggested that she fear him, but her heart and her guts...

"Do you want me to take you back home, Valli?" he asked.

She just stared at him. Emotional. Confused. His question wasn't at all what she'd been expecting when she'd agreed to be alone with him. She'd assumed he'd not only try and get her to stay, but attempt to convince her to let Jean-Baptiste take down those barriers he believed the doctors at the clinic had placed in her mind.

"And if I say yes?" she challenged. Why wasn't she yanking her hand away? Why wasn't his touch revolting to her?

"Then I'll take you."

His full lips formed a gentle smile, which was really a feat because he was such a formidable man, such a strikingly handsome, intimidating, proud man.

"I would just ask..." he began.

Bitterness instantly rose within her. She knew it wouldn't be that easy, that simple. In her experience, her past, men always wanted something for—

"That you let me be there for you if you need anything," he said. "And for the cub. The child."

She stilled. And something started to hurt behind her eyes. It wasn't a headache or sinus pain, but the pressure was intense. "I don't understand you," she whispered, her throat tight. "I don't understand any of this."

A soft gust of wind came through the open window behind her. It ruffled his blond hair.

His eyes clung to hers, desperate to connect. "I was in the clinic too, Valli," he said in an intimate voice. "But in a very different way. For a different purpose."

"What do you mean?" she asked, confused.

"Not to get well, like you." His eyes shuttered with pain. "But to be used for my blood. Many of us were taken from here, from our homes, our families, to be caged, beaten, drugged and bled."

It was as if the air in the room had suddenly been sucked out. Valli stared at the man, wordless, her pulse starting to pound in her head.

"To them," he continued. "Me and my kind aren't worthy of respect or care. To them, we have no choice or freedom. To them, we're animals...like you said..."

"Stop!" Valli shook her head. This was a nightmare. All of it. She'd just wanted to live. She hadn't thought... Christ, she hadn't cared about who might suffer for that gift. "I'm so sorry," she whispered. "I'm so sorry."

Blade cursed and squeezed her hand, and this time her heart took over and she squeezed back.

"You don't have to be sorry," he said. "According to what they put in your mind, what they forced you to believe—I am an animal."

Tears threatened and her heart ached terribly. "I want the best for this baby and for myself. I just want the truth." Her eyes implored him. "How do I know what that is? How do I know it's not more lies?"

"Put my hand on your abdomen."

"What? Why?"

"Please," he said gently.

Valli hesitated. Holding his hand was one thing... But she didn't like men touching her.

Her eyes met his and the warmth, the hope in them spoke to every inch of her.

She lifted his hand and gently placed it on her belly. She was only two months along, barely showing, just a slight curve.

She watched as Blade's eyes closed, his nostrils flared, and a soft growl exited his throat. The sound should've made her nervous, made her push his hand from her stomach, but it had the opposite effect. It was the most comforting feeling she had ever known.

And then it happened.

Beneath his hand, and deep within her.

The slightest movement. A tiny ripple of feeling.

His eyes opened and locked with hers, hot and blissful.

"Our cub knows me," he rasped.

Tears broke from her eyes then. She couldn't contain them. Didn't want to.

He eased his hand from her belly and reached up, cupping her face, his thumb caressing her cheek. "Valli, I've never touched you until last night. But I was in the room with you. They had me in there, drugged and tied down. I was forced to watch as they put my seed inside of you. I couldn't move, couldn't stop them, couldn't protect you—" His voice cracked and he pulled his hand from her and stood up. As she watched, he turned and gave her his back. "It will be my greatest shame for as long as I live."

Tears snaked down Valli's cheeks. She'd never felt this raw. She'd never felt such a desperate need to believe someone.

He started for the door. "I'm going to tell Baptiste that I'm taking you home."

"No!" she shouted, her heart pounding so hard she was afraid her ribs were bruising.

Blade froze, his hand on the door handle.

"Bring him back in here," she said, swiping at her wet cheeks. "Tell him I want his help. I want to see what happened. I want the truth. And as far as going home is concerned..."

Her voice broke as he turned to look at her. She'd never seen a man so conflicted.

Or so ruthlessly handsome.

"I don't know where *I* belong, but this child clearly believes it's home."

Chapter 5

Jean-Baptiste, the Pantera Healer, was tall, dark and terrifying. In fact, he looked like he should be wearing leather and carrying a sawed-off shotgun, not a lab coat and stethoscope. But Valli was starting to understand this race of shifters. They were imposing and possessive, but like Blade, they were also kind and compassionate—and protective.

Tattoos and bulging muscles, the Healer moved to stand next to the bed, a gentle concern radiating in his amber eyes.

"Are you ready?"

Her heart leapt into her throat, but she gave a small nod. "Yes."

He reached for a wooden chair and set it next to the headboard. Then, with a quick glance toward Blade, who was sitting close beside her on the mattress, he placed his hand on her forehead. It was warm and soothing and...

Untamed?

No, that wasn't her. It was Blade's raw emotion. She sensed him stiffen beside her, but before she could ask him what was wrong, she felt a deep sense of peace flow through her.

Magic?

Who knew?

But it felt like it.

"I want you to close your eyes," Jean-Baptiste requested softly. "Tell me what you remember about your time in the clinic."

Instinctively, Valli reached out to grab Blade's hand. She'd tried so hard not to think about the clinic or what had happened there. What she'd allowed to happen. What she'd taken that didn't belong to her.

Because it was the only way she could face the future once she'd realized she was pregnant.

Now she needed Blade's strength if she was going to be forced to relive the horror she now one hundred percent believed was a part of her past. And her child's conception.

As if sensing her unease, Blade moved so his hip was pressed against her thigh, his fingers squeezing her hand.

It was an unspoken promise that he was there to protect her. And he wasn't going anywhere.

Slowly closing her eyes, Valli allowed the Healer's magic to fully take hold. She felt a strange sensation behind her eyes, as if her mind was a safe and a soft key was being gently thrust into the lock.

"Oh God…I'm growing weaker and weaker," she began. "It started small. Just a shakiness in my legs when I finished my evening shift. And then…" She swallowed tightly. "I started dropping things, trays, cups. I managed to hide it for a while. As long as I could. But eventually Fran started to notice. She was great… Made me take time off. But I didn't get better. I just slept and slept." Her voice broke slightly. "I could barely climb out of bed in the morning."

A rush of soothing warmth moved from her forehead downward, and Blade started to massage her hand.

"Dr. Richards had nothing for me, no diagnosis for this strange, horrible, debilitating illness. I was scared and started to get really depressed. I didn't feel like I had anyone to turn to. Then one day, the doctor told me he knew about this place, this clinic. He felt it could help me. I hoped he'd take me there himself, but he said he was too busy with all of his patients. I didn't want to inconvenience Fran by asking her, not with having only one waitress left at the diner. So I dragged myself on that bus to Benson's clinic in Baton Rouge."

Valli could hear her voice shaking, but couldn't seem to stop it. It was just so vivid, the exhaustion, the fear, and then that burst of hope she'd felt when she'd first arrived.

"It all seemed so high tech there," she continued. "And the staff made me feel like I was going to be okay, when I just felt like I was on the edge of death. Then…" Valli shook her head against what came next. "The doctors told me the only cure to what I had was a transfusion of Pantera blood."

For one brief second, the soothing warmth at her temples cooled, then quickly returned.

"I didn't know," she uttered, pained. "I didn't even really believe in the Pantera. I thought it was a hoax, a conspiracy theory. But honestly, in that moment, I didn't care. I was on the verge of death and I would've done anything to live."

Blade squeezed her hand reassuringly.

"The effect was immediate," she went on, her tone almost euphoric to her own ears. "It was amazing. I was so grateful. I wanted to believe that the clinic was a gift from the heavens. I wanted to ignore the warning bells clanging inside of my head. I wanted to forget they'd used another's blood on me. And that it belonged to an animal. And..." At last her words faltered.

Jean-Baptiste's hand left her forehead and brushed down her cheek, sending a warm sensation of peace through her body.

"Can you tell me about the day you believe you were attacked by Blade?" Jean-Baptiste urged in gentle tones.

This time, it was Valli's turn to squeeze Blade's hand tighter. Despite the Healer's magic, she could feel her muscles tensing and her stomach twisting as she tried to struggle past the darkness of her heart and the dark holes in her memory.

"I knew I was scheduled for another transfusion," she said in a tentative voice, the curtain of her mind starting to lift. "I asked the nurse why I had to have another one since I was feeling so much better."

"Were you in a private room for the transfusion?" the Healer asked.

Even though her insides were humming with nerves, Valli forced herself to concentrate on what her mind was showing her, the fragments, trying to piece them together.

She'd had breakfast. Biscuits and gravy. She'd put too much salt on the gravy. Then she'd wanted to take a walk through the nearby park. It'd been so long since she'd felt strong enough to go out on her own that she was anxious to enjoy a short stroll.

Heat surged through her as her mind suddenly opened and she saw...and remembered.

Oh God...

Four lab techs in white uniforms had arrived in her room, along with the nurse.

"They put me on a gurney and wheeled me to the lab," she whispered.

"Did they give you anything?"

She frowned at Jean-Baptiste's question. "What do you mean?"

"Any drugs? Injections of any kind," he clarified.

"No. I don't think so." She'd been surprised during her first days at the clinic. She'd assumed that she would be put on a wide range of pills in an attempt to find a cure for her mysterious illness. But the doctors had immediately prescribed the transfusions.

Jean-Baptiste released another pulse of warmth through his hand, and her breath caught in her throat. "Wait." Her vision cleared. She could suddenly see it, being wheeled down the green-tiled corridor with a needle stuck in her arm. "I had an IV."

"Was that unusual?"

"They gave me IVs during the actual transfusions, but never before or after," she said. "But this one had a clear fluid in it."

Fear snaked down Valli's spine and she shivered. It was all so clear now. Like a vault opening... She could see everything from every angle. Whereas before, after she'd left the clinic and up until a few minutes ago, it was like...pictures in a picture frame.

She could remember being troubled by the changes to her normal routine, as if she'd had a premonition that something sinister was about to happen.

"So they took you to the lab." Jean-Baptiste kept his voice soothing. No doubt he sensed the panic that was beginning to nibble at the edge of her mind. "Were you the only patient in there?"

She licked her lips. She didn't want to see it...or know it. But she had to. *The past can't hurt you*, she reassured herself. *Not anymore.*

Forcing herself to take a deep breath, she concentrated on the memory, of being wheeled into the lab, letting it unfold like scenes from a movie.

It'd been cold in the room and she'd shivered. She'd been in a hospital gown that was too thin to keep her warm, and her requests for a blanket had been ignored.

They'd situated her in the middle of the room, beneath a light that had been blinding in its intensity. She'd turned her head to avoid the brightness and realized that there was a gurney just a foot away from her.

"There was someone next to me," she rasped, her heart racing. "I assumed it was another patient who was there for a transfusion."

Jean-Baptiste continued to lightly stroke his fingers over her face. "Did you see who it was?"

Her pulse pounded in her throat as she suddenly relived the moment. No longer was it in the past, safe, behind her. It was happening now. "I'm starting to feel the effects of whatever they've given me. It's gentle, a sedative, maybe." She saw the gurney and the outline of a large man. He turned his head. Oh God... The stark beauty of Blade's face.

She gasped.

It burned into her brain as she stared at him. Every line and curve. And those dark eyes... They held hers. So angry, so pained...desperate...

"Blade," she breathed.

"He's on the gurney?" Jean-Baptiste demanded even as Blade's fingers gripped her hand with a fierce strength.

"Yes," she said.

"Is he restrained?" the Healer asked.

Valli paused. It'd always been easy to remember Blade's face, as if it'd been such a life-altering sight that nothing could erase it. But the rest of the memories surrounding him had been shattered and shrouded in darkness. Now she felt a layer of perspiration dampen her forehead as she strained to piece her past back together.

Slowly she could make out the details of Blade's large, powerful body. He was huge, tall and broad, and wearing a hospital gown that matched hers. He was lying on his back. His arms were stretched over his head and his legs were parted.

"Oh." She released a shocked breath. "I can see the iron cuffs on his wrists and ankles."

"Malachite," Blade muttered.

She ignored his interruption, still lost in the memories that were coming faster and faster.

"He's trying to escape," she said, now able to clearly remember his body undulating like a wild animal that had been caught in a trap. "He's trying to get to me..." Her voice broke again and she felt tears behind her eyes. "He's trying to help me."

How had she forgotten his low grunts of pain as he'd fought against his restraints?

Had she just confused his furious attempts to free himself with the doctor's claim that she'd been attacked by an animal and raped?

Oh, God...

Jean-Baptiste's hand moved to the back of her head, pressing against the dull ache that she hadn't even realized was beginning to form.

"Keep going, Valli," he urged. "It's okay."

Blade was struggling, growling, fighting. And she felt...confused. She wanted to speak, but a fine mist was starting to cloud her eyes. It wasn't the darkness that had prevented her from remembering what she saw now, but a physical reaction to something that had been done to her.

"Things are starting to get really fuzzy. Heavier sedation, maybe?" She hesitated, still lost in the past. She'd been trying to focus on the man restrained in the gurney next to her when the sound of the door to the lab opening and closing had her turning her head. Groggily, she saw a familiar man and woman walking toward her. "I can see my doctors coming toward me," she said, suddenly making a sound of distress as the lab techs reached down to grab her.

"Valli." Blade leaned toward her, his breath brushing her cheek. "I'm here. No one can hurt you. I'll never let anyone hurt you again."

Jean-Baptiste also moved closer, his hand on her head. Any other time she would have felt like she was being smothered by the sizzling power that was pressing against her. Now she ached, silently begged, for the comforting heat.

"What's happening?" Jean-Baptiste demanded.

Valli started to shake her head. Over and over. "No, no, no..."

"Valli," Blade whispered.

"They're forcing my legs apart and strapping me down." Her words came out as a low cry. "I'm trying to fight. Can't...too weak. They're putting something inside... Oh my God, no... Why are they doing this?"

"Enough!" Blade rasped, his arms sliding around her as he hauled her trembling body toward him. "Oh, *ma chère*, I'm so sorry. Goddess help me. I'm so sorry you had to go through that."

Tears rolling down her cheeks, she pressed herself hard against his chest, savoring his intoxicating musk.

"It wasn't you," she breathed, her arms wrapping tightly around his neck. "It was never you."

He buried his face in the curve of her neck. "It's over now, *ma chère*. No one will ever hurt you again. I swear it on my life."

Chapter 6

Never had Blade felt so protective of another being. He was a Pantera, and that made him a natural defender, but this female, and the life growing inside of her, well, they brought out something close to feral in his heart.

And in his cat.

After they'd shared a quick meal of soup and bread, Blade had shown Valli to the room where she'd be staying, for how long he didn't know. He did know the hope he had in his heart, of course, but he would never force the issue. He'd been caged for too long. He'd never do that to another. But he wanted her to be as comfortable as possible.

He wanted her to see it as a home.

He'd given her the room on the other side of the cottage. It was fresh and clean, with pale yellow bed covers, white curtains, and a soft oval rug on the floor. It also faced the gardens and a heavy stand of cypress. She'd smiled when she saw it, and she'd settled in, he'd almost told her she could have it redone any way she wanted.

But he'd held his tongue.

Blade poured two glasses of sweet tea and headed for the front door. At the screen, he paused. Valli was sitting in one of the chairs on the porch. In the light of the coming sunset, her sable hair glowed as it fell about her bare shoulders. She was the most beautiful female he'd ever known, and all he wanted to do was sit beside her and take her hand in his.

It was so strange, this feeling. He'd never known it or wanted it. He liked to travel, get away, not be tied down. And yet, here he was dreaming about porches and holding hands—

A sound rent the calm bayou air, ripping him from his fantasy. Like feet pounding earth.

No, not feet.

Those were the heavy pads of a puma on a mission.

Blade pushed the screen door open and stepped out onto the porch, just as Valli pointed toward the feline weaving through the cypress at a quick pace. She stood up and the pale yellow cat with crystal blue eyes headed straight for them.

What did she want?

Setting the tea down on a nearby table, Blade stepped to the edge of the porch, directly in front of Valli. He didn't want anyone around tonight, especially a former colleague. He wanted Valli all to himself.

In seconds the cat transformed into the female he knew well. Or had known... But that was a long time ago.

"Good to see you back, Blade."

He gave her a nod. "Good to be back." He glanced over his shoulder. Valli looked stunned. She'd clearly never seen a shift, and the surprise at both the act and the fact that Pantera are fully clothed when they do, had her eyes bulging. "Valli, this is Faith. A fellow Suit."

"Right," Faith drawled. "Just a fellow Suit."

Blade did not have the time or the energy to deal with this female's age-old and very one-sided crush. "What do you want, Faith?"

She was staring at Valli, or trying to. "Houseguest?" she drawled.

Before he could get a word out, Valli came to stand beside him. She was trembling slightly, but her chin was high and her eyes never left the female's. "It's nice to meet you, Faith."

The Pantera female's nostrils flared and her eyes dropped to Valli's abdomen.

That's right. My cub. My female.

"You, too." This time when Faith's gaze lifted, her expression was far more gentle and respectful. "Sorry I scared the shit out of you."

"You didn't," Valli said. "It was just...surprising."

"Of course." Faith gave her a halfhearted smile. "I'm sure you'll get used to it. The longer you're around us...and then with your own cub—"

Blade cut her off. Again. "What do you need, Faith?"

Faith flicked a brow upward, her sky-blue eyes darting between Blade and Valli. "Okaaay...Raph sent me."

"And?"

"He wants to see you first thing in the morning."

A thread of irritation moved through Blade. "He could've called or texted me."

"I was in the office," she said casually. "I volunteered."

Blade sensed it was more than that. He suspected that this female Pantera who'd once had feelings for him wanted to check out the human female who'd brought him back home to the Wildlands when nothing else ever had.

"Well, thanks for the message," he told her, slipping his arm around Valli. "It was good to see you, Faith. Have a good night."

The message was loud and clear, and Faith took it in stride. She gave them both a nod, then turned around and raced off, shifting back into her puma by the time she hit the stand of cypress.

Alone once again, Blade turned to Valli and gave her an apologetic smile. "I'm sorry about that."

"Don't be. It really was just surprising." She inhaled deeply, glancing out at the sunset. "And it's me who's sorry, Blade. About everything. Accusing you, fearing you."

"You had no choice, Valli. What they did to you... You've suffered too much."

She turned back to look at him. "No more than you suffered. I can't imagine the pain you endured."

His chest tightened at her words and the way she looked at him—a strange combination of hope and need and apprehension. He wanted to give her the first two and take away the last.

"We're here now," he said. "You're safe, surrounded by those who wish us good health and happiness."

"Like Faith?"

His lips twitched, but he nodded.

"She knew I was pregnant."

"She scented it."

Her lips flattened and a just a hint of fire illuminated her eyes. "And she didn't seem happy about it. She did, however, seem into you."

Blade smiled and took her hands in his. "She was happy. We're family here, Valli. And we haven't seen cubs born to our kind in a very long time. It's a miracle that each of us thanks the Goddess for. Now... Faith might've had a crush on me, but that was a long time ago."

Her eyes searched his. "Did you have a crush on her too?"

Heat surged through him. His human female was showing her interest, staking her claim. And nothing could've made him happier in that moment. "Never. In fact," he added. "I've never had a crush… until now."

Her cheeks grew pink and she smiled softly. "Tell me about yourself, your life here. Do you have blood relations? Immediate family? Parents? Siblings?"

"I actually never knew my parents," he told her. "I think they're living in Europe somewhere." He turned and looked at the dying sunset over the bayou. "It's what I heard when I was a cub, anyway. I was actually raised by my grandmother, but she's long passed."

"Was she good to you?"

He glanced back at her, thoughtful. "She was strict, but very, very loving."

She exhaled. "You're lucky."

It was the first time Blade had wondered about her history, her family. With none of his own, he'd been thinking only of the future. What they could create together.

"I saw that you were living at the diner," he said. "Is the woman who owns it your relative?"

"She's a friend." Her eyes searched his. "I'm kind of like you. Absent parents."

"I don't want that for our cub, Valli," Blade said impulsively.

Her eyes widened and her lips parted. For a moment, Blade had to rein in the temptation to kiss her. Her scent alone stirred his blood.

"I've heard you say that a few times," she said. "Cub?"

"It's what we call our young."

"Do you think…"

"What?"

"The baby will be able to…"

"Shift?" he supplied with a smile.

She returned it softly. "Must be wonderful to shed your human skin. Be something else. Run on instinct. Do you shift a lot?"

He shook his head. "Haven't in several weeks. We can only shift inside the Wildlands. The magic won't stretch farther. And since I returned last night, I haven't had the chance."

Her eyes suddenly clouded. "So you couldn't shift when you were held captive? All that time..."

Blade didn't answer. He released her hands and went to the edge of the porch, looking out at his beloved Wildlands. "It was torture at times. The urge was there, the hunger, but no way to satisfy it."

"Like sex?"

His ire receded, and a smile touched his lips. "A little bit like that, yes."

She came up beside him. "Can I see, Blade?"

"What?" He turned to look at her.

Her eyes were wide and her cheeks were flushed. "Do you want to do it right now?"

Blade's skin went tight around his muscles and his cock filled with blood. "Valli..."

"What color is it?" she interrupted. "Is it fierce? Would it hurt me?"

Even as Blade grew impossibly hard, he knew she wasn't talking about sex. She was talking about his cat. That's what she wanted. Wanted to see.

Disappointment swept over him, but he refused to give in to it. If the female wanted to see his puma, he would show it to her. After all, it belonged to her, it would be ruled by her someday. Not that she knew that.

He gave her a wicked grin, then leapt over the porch railing. Once he was a few feet away he turned back to her and called, "Don't be scared, female. It would never hurt you. In fact, it would kill to save you and the cub."

Her eyes glittered with interest. "Show me."

Your wish is our command.

Closing his eyes, Blade called upon his cat. With weeks passing since he'd last worn fur, the feline was right below the surface of his skin. Desperate to emerge. Instantly, he felt the hum of the shift, felt his bones change and reform, his muscles too. And then, there was only peace and instinct.

Life was just that simple inside the cat.

It wanted only basic things. Food, sunlight, exercise, mating... His eyes opened. Valli.

With a soft growl, he padded toward the porch, letting her look him over. From massive head to flickering tail. Letting the curiosity in her expression morph into amazement, and something else...

Desire?

No, that wasn't possible. Not yet.

Drawn to her, he leapt over the very railing he'd jumped a moment ago as a male and stalked over to her, rubbing against her legs. She was a tall female, and it was easy to position his head beneath her hand.

"So beautiful," she uttered, her voice threaded with awe.

As she petted him, long heavy strokes from his head to his lower back, the scent of her mixed sublimely with the scent of his young. It flooded his puma's nostrils and brought on a low, warm growl from deep in his throat. Without thought, only instinct, the cat turned into her and rubbed its massive face against her lower abdomen.

Mine.

As if she'd heard him, a soft sound escaped Valli's throat. Nostrils flaring, his puma pulled in the delectable bloom of her arousal. The cat eased its head back, glancing up. Gone was the smile. Valli looked pink and wonderfully turned on. But her eyes were humming with unease. Maybe she wasn't sure if she should feel what she was feeling.

His cat didn't like the look and pulled its head from her warm hand. Calling the feline home, Blade quickly shifted back into his male form.

Valli was breathing shallowly now, and even without the cat he scented her arousal.

"I..." she began, licking her lips.

"Valli—"

"I should go to bed." She swallowed and clarified, "To sleep. I... Good night." Then she turned around and disappeared inside the house.

* * * *

Something was definitely wrong with her.

After changing into the cotton shorts and white tank that had been donated by a female in town—along with several other lovely things with the tags still on them—Valli dropped back on the bed and pulled the covers up to her waist.

When Blade's cat had nuzzled her belly...

She dropped her head, her cheeks on fire.

Such a feeling. Like nothing she'd ever experienced—or even imagined existed. Not only was there an assault of heat everywhere inside her body, but the euphoric sensation of utter bliss. Like that moment, that action, was what life was all about.

Oh, God, she sounded like a crazy person. A Pantera puma rubbed up against her a little bit. It wasn't the height of eroticism. Or shouldn't be.

And yet, it was.

She stared up at the ceiling as a cool, fragrant breeze wafted through the open window to her left. Was this undeniable attraction about guilt? Did she feel guilty about treating him so badly? Accusing him of assaulting her? Was her mind trying to turn the negative into a positive connection with the father of her child?

The answers to her silent questions never came, but a knock on the door sure did.

"Valli?"

Her heart shot up into her throat and she tossed off the covers and sat up. Lord, his voice was so dark and arresting. It made her feel restless. Again.

She went over to the door and leaned against it. She didn't dare open it. She was rattled, aroused, and she didn't want him to see it. Or, heaven help her, smell it.

"Do you have everything you need?" he asked through the wood.

Hell no. You're out there and I'm in here.

"Yes, thanks."

A long silence followed, then, "Okay. Then..sleep well."

"You, too, Blade."

As she turned from the door, she thought she heard a low rumble of a growl, but she couldn't be sure.

Disappointment snaked through her. At him, and at herself. Why hadn't she just opened the stupid door? So he might've scented her attraction. Big deal. They didn't have to do anything about it. They could've talked a bit more. Shared some coffee or dessert.

Or a passionate kiss where he held her against his chest and put his big hands on the back of her head, threading his fingers in her hair.

She fell back on the bed and heaved a sigh. Yes, something was definitely wrong with her.

What was she going to do? She couldn't stay here. She had a job and a life and an apartment. Well, she prayed she did. She hadn't called Fran yet, hadn't wanted to lie about where she was or tell the truth of it—but no doubt the woman was beyond worried. She had to go back.

She had to be able to support her child, because no matter how attracted she was to this Pantera male, she wouldn't allow herself to get pulled into something that very well might be a short-lived whatever. He'd come after her because she carried his child, and she needed to keep reminding herself of that.

Men don't stick around.

If she'd learned anything from her sorry excuse for a mother, it was that. They get what they came for and take off.

Blade's face appeared in her mind. Those soulful and fierce black eyes, the sharp cheekbones and full lips. Instantly, her stupid insides melted again. It was crazy. Ever since she and this male had talked in the Panteras' infirmary, she'd felt impossibly drawn to him, like she'd seen his heart, open and honest. And now, since coming to his home, all she wanted to do was be touched by him.

Was it the child?

The cub.

The word made her smile softly. She was never going to sleep tonight.

A scent wafted through the open window then. Bayou and flowers, and wet, green earth, and night. And...something else.

She inhaled deeply. Whatever it was, it was so intoxicating that when it entered her lungs, a rush of heat spread throughout her entire body.

She'd been sexual with only one man in her life. It wasn't a long-term thing, and after a few months he'd revealed he'd been seeing someone else on the side. So over the years, she'd gotten used to taking care of her own needs. She'd wanted to make sure she was never dependent on a man for pleasure. Or anything else. Because once you were, you gave up your power.

The scent hit her nostrils again. Spicy and hot...

Groaning, she slipped her hand inside the waistband of her shorts and ran it down her pelvis until she met shaved, warm skin. Her eyes closed and Blade appeared in her mind. There he was. Shifting from man to beast and back again. So powerful, so protective.

The image made her instantly wet and she slipped her fingers inside her folds and found her clit.

A groan exited her lips as her ear picked up a strange sound. She froze for a moment and listened. Something was outside, but not close.

It was moving in the brush.

Pulling her hand from her body, she leapt from the bed and went to the window. At first, all she saw was cypress and the garden in the dark of night. But then she caught movement again and tracked it. Several yards away, under the bright glow of moonlight, an amber cat stalked something.

Long, purposeful, predatory strides.

Blade.

Her sex clenched with need. Maybe it was the Wildlands, the magic they possessed. Maybe they were possessing her.

Or, goddamit, maybe she just wanted this male.

Without sense or reason, she stripped off all her clothes and stood at the window naked. As she watched him chase something in the stand of cypress, her hands cupped her breasts. Massaging them, she whimpered. Tugging and playing with her hard nipples, she thrust her hips forward.

Releasing one of her breasts, she drew her hand down over her small curve of belly and straight for the spot that ached for her touch.

Or his.

Her fingers circled her clit slowly, drawing in the warm wetness. God, she wanted him inside of her. Over her, behind her, on his knees before her...

A groan escaped her lips.

The sound floated out, into the woodland.

And within the heavy brush, the cat froze, turned its massive head and saw her.

Valli inhaled sharply. *Move. Get back to bed. Don't let him see you!*

But she didn't listen to her inner voice. Not this time. Boldly, brashly, she remained.

The cat drew closer, eyes narrowed, nostrils flared, and she stared at it, her fingers now moving again.

For a moment, the cat stilled, drew up on his hind legs, tipped his head back and scented the air. In seconds, a growl unlike anything Valli had ever heard before rent the air. It was a feral, hungry, possessive sound.

And it nearly made her come.

Her eyes locked to his, to the puma, she whispered the words, "Blade, please."

No doubt the male didn't hear it, couldn't. But his cat did. The massive creature started for her, paws pounding the earth, running with elegant, predatory grace, stopping only when it was a few feet away.

To shift.

It was like something out of a dream: man emerging from beast, stripping naked, coming at her highly aroused. Nearly flying to the window, his eyes closing and his voice rough as he said those four little words that made her breath catch and her heart sore.

"Can I come in?"

Chapter 7

Blade wanted her on the bed. Her back to the mattress. Her legs open. Her pussy glistening. And her clit pink and swollen.

But it was too damn far away.

The scent of her was crying out to him, begging for his mouth, his tongue, his teeth...

He eased her back against the wall and spread her legs with his thigh. Then he dropped to his knees before her. When his cat had seen her through the window, and when the scent of her self-pleasure had reached its nostrils, the puma had gone insane.

Mine, it growled.

Ours, Blade had corrected.

But there was no talking to the feline or trying to reason with it. Not from the male part of him, the part that wanted the very same thing.

"Did you hear me say your name?" she whispered breathlessly.

He glanced up, struck once again by her beauty. So tall, with long, exquisite legs, rounded hips, a curve of belly that housed his cub, breasts that made his mouth water, and eyes that humbled him.

"We both did," he said with a hint of a snarl.

She smiled secretively. Sensually.

Desire raged through him and his hands went around her to squeeze her very fine ass. But his eyes stayed on hers. "What are you thinking, female?" he demanded.

She sucked air between her teeth and her nipples hardened. "I like it. Your cat."

"Well, it likes you, too. More than you can ever imagine." A growl rumbled in his throat, and he leaned in and kissed the top of her shaved pussy. "Valli," he whispered against the warm, wet flesh. "If you don't want me to devour you right now, make you tremble and cry out, tell me to get the fuck out of here and never come back."

He waited. Dying of thirst, nearly going mad, he waited.

But she didn't say a word. Instead, she reached for him, her fingers threading in his short blond hair, her palms finding the back of his head. And with a soft sigh, she eased him closer to her sex.

It was all Blade needed. He snarled with hunger, then ran his tongue up the seam of her pussy, just to get a hint of her on his taste buds. Goddess, he wanted to remember, he wanted to savor, his first time with Valli, with his ma—

Her groan of satisfaction drowned out his thought. That wild thought. That rogue thought.

That fucking delicious thought.

With one hand cupping her ass, he slid the other one down and slipped two fingers deep inside of her.

A soft groan escaped her and she gripped his head even tighter, her nails slightly scraping his scalp. The reaction made him crazy with lust and he buried his face in her, flattening his tongue on her clit, covering it completely. And with slow, methodical jerks upward, he urged her into heavy pants of desire and jerky thrusts of her hips.

Mine. All mine.

"Blade," she rasped. "Oh, God."

His marble-hard cock pressed against his belly as he ate her, his seed leaking at the tip. It was as it should be. He was a Pantera male. Taking his female. Feeding from her. Nourishing his body and soul as he pleasured his...

A strange shock of emotion washed over him and he released her, drew back from her drenched pussy.

His eyes lifted and once again he took in her beauty. Her eyes were wild, her lips were parted and her face was flushed. She was watching him, her brows furrowed, her breathing labored.

"What's wrong?" she uttered. "Did I do something—"

"No, *ma chère*," he said quickly, fiercely. "Goddess, no. You are the sweetest, most incredible gift." His nostrils flared. "You have no idea...what this means to me. What you mean..."

His words faltered as his chest went tight with an emotion he'd never believed he'd ever possess.

Valli bent down then, crouched before him, her face close to his, her eyes searching his for answers.

"Talk to me," she urged. "Please."

For a moment, Blade wanted to rebuke himself. Pantera males suppressed emotion, especially ones that contained any sentimentality. But he feared if he didn't allow this one, it would come out in ways that weren't conducive to holding on to a female and a cub.

He reached up and brushed a stray strand of hair from her face, tucking it behind her ear. "This is the first time in many, many years," he began, "that my hard cock spills its seed from true hunger and desire, not a medical procedure or drug."

She gasped. "Oh, God, Blade." She reached out and took his face in her hands. "I'm so horribly sorry. I should've never—"

"Valli," he cut her off. "No. No, *ma chère*. You misunderstand my reaction. I'm not upset and I sure as hell don't want to stop. I'm grateful. I want more. I want this to never fucking end. I want to touch you, kiss you, lick you, make love to you every day of my life." His eyes met hers. "Don't you see, female? Freedom is all the more beautiful because you're in it with me."

Tears filled her eyes. Wide, stunned, beautiful eyes. "Blade."

He leaned in and claimed her mouth, as he wanted to claim her. As his mate. As the mother of his cub. Slow, drugging, passion-filled kisses that had his heart slamming against his ribs and his fingers finding her swollen clit once again.

As he stroked her, he took each moan into his mouth and played it with his tongue. The sounds she made and the scent that filled the air between them called out to his cat, and once again he was the predator, all softness gone. His one goal was to hear her scream with pleasure, and when it happened—when he took her there, his fingers playing her swollen bud until she cried out over and over, until sweet, wet cream soaked his hand, he finally knew true happiness.

And the truest hunger.

He stood up and swept her into his arms. "I'm taking you to bed, Valli."

* * * *

Heart beating frantically, eyes pinned to the male poised above her, Valli felt a shocking sense of possessiveness. And who could blame her? Blade was truly a sight to behold.

Powerful, hard body...every lean inch of it...with wide imposing shoulders and a ruggedly beautiful face that spoke of ageless strength.

Her male.

And her child's father.

The truth of both of those thoughts sent her hands to his chest, raking upward to his shoulders and around to his back, which was all ropes of sinewy muscle.

With one thick thigh, Blade eased her legs apart, and as Valli watched with breath-stealing excitement, he brought his massive cock to her pussy and entered her so slowly, inch by glorious inch, until she sucked in air. Until she was so was deliriously full she had no words, no thoughts.

Only hunger.

And need.

"Goddess, you feel like heaven," Blade said, his eyes never leaving hers as he remained buried deep inside of her. "My heaven."

Wrapping her legs around his waist, Valli pulled him even closer with a quick thrust. The movement made her gasp, then smile. She wanted to feel his weight on her, his mouth on her. She wanted everything. It was the strangest sensation. Almost manic.

And she loved it.

Blade's expression was dark as he loomed over her. "I don't want to hurt the cub."

Her smile widened. "You won't."

He dropped his head and kissed her, soft and hungry. "Or you."

She lapped at his lower lip with her tongue. "You never could. You promised, remember?"

"Always, Valli." His eyes were deadly serious now. "Always."

As he started to move inside her, every stroke, every deep thrust, a blissful surprise to her system, it was as though they were one—it was as though they were creating their child—their cub—in the real way. The way it should've been.

Eyes pinned to his, heat raged through Valli. Never had she felt like this, so taken, so filled. And yet so free. Blade wanted nothing from her but her pleasure, and he made her heart squeeze and her mind soften until all that was left of her were nerve endings and tight muscles and the groans of his pleasure in her ear.

Was this what women talked about in groups, bragged about to their less fortunate friends, searched for every damn day of their lives?

To be taken so completely?

Where every inch of themselves, inside and out, was hovering on the brink of utter and complete satisfaction?

The question died as Blade drove deep into her, then held there, As his mouth took hers, consuming her with slow, drugging kisses, he thrust up, settling his pelvis snug against her sensitive clit. In quick, small movements, he fucked both her pussy and her swollen bud. Over and over and over until...

Valli cried out against his mouth. It was too much. And yet not enough. Never enough. Blade. Her man. She gripped onto his back, her nails digging into his thickly muscled skin as wave upon wave of climax assaulted her.

Blade growled into her ear and nipped at her lobe. "Goddess, Valli, you're so tight. The way you hold my cock... And yet, I need to stretch you further."

"Yes," she whispered, again and again as the last crashes of orgasm slashed through her.

Blade snarled and groaned as he thrust in and out, deep, so deep... "You're mine, Valli! Mine... Don't ever forget that."

Never.

Eyes open now, Valli watched him, her magnificent beast, as she held on tight. His climax was so feral, his seed so deliciously hot she wished it was going down her dry throat. Filling her. Filling her in ways she could only have dreamt about before this night.

How had she thought life existed before now?

Before him.

Them.

And then he was rolling to the side and taking her with him. Still deep, still hard, still attached. Growling softly as he pulled her close.

Instantly, wonderfully, Valli curled into him, feeling—for the first time in her life—warm and safe. She never wanted to let go. She never wanted this feeling to end.

But as their bodies started to cool, a strange sensation crept over her, like a cool, damp blanket. Thoughts snaked into her mind...fears...of trusting this wonderful male. Any male, after what she'd seen and experienced as a child... Fears of not being able to give herself to Blade any more than she already had. With her heart and soul. No matter how much she wanted to. Fear that she was too damaged...to love him, her child...the way they deserved...

Stop. Just stop.

With a growl of her own, she pushed the dark negativity away, then shoved Blade to his back. She knew what she felt. Knew this was different and special. And she would not allow the devils of her past to steal her light, her rainbows...

Her glorious time with this man.

A slow smile on her lips, she crawled on top of him. He remained hard as stone, his cock standing up, glistening and ready for her again. Fire raged in his eyes as he watched her mount him.

Enjoy what's being given to you, Valli. For however long it lasts.

But as she sank down on his marble length, took him fully, saw the puma flash in his eyes, everything inside of her whispered...

Mine.

Forever.

Chapter 8

Except for the daily medical checkup, they'd hardly left the bed in the last three days, and even now he wanted back in. Hell, he never wanted to leave her again. Not even for a second. But Blade had been called to Headquarters to report on Valli's progress with Raphael. He'd had a brief, crazy desire to decline the invitation.

Thankfully, he wasn't suicidal.

No one said no to the leader of the Suits. Not if they wanted to keep their manly parts intact. Besides, he understood Raphael's need to be assured that the Healers had declared Valli healthy and untainted by the time she'd spent in Benson's clinic. Not to mention to make sure the cub was growing well.

Done and done.

Now, as he stepped out of the sprawling Headquarters and shifted into his puma form, gliding through the cypress trees, he felt wonderfully alive and happy for the first time in as far back as he could remember. His large paws padded on the mossy ground with lethal silence, his tail twitching, while around him the wetland was stirring to life as the morning sun crested the horizon to spill a golden warmth through the thick canopy of leaves.

It felt glorious to release his cat, absorbing the magic that surrounded him. But as much as he enjoyed spending the morning running through the bayou, nostrils flared and on the hunt for prey, he had someone waiting for him at home.

Home.

For the first time in his life, his small cottage wasn't just a place to sleep when he wasn't traveling around the world.

Now it was filled with his female and soon-to-be cub.

He was already considering how he could build on a new kitchen and playroom, not to mention filling it with new furniture and frilly curtains.

Bypassing the communal center, he loped down the narrow trail, pausing to resume his human form before he was in sight of his cottage. Valli was starting to get used to being surrounded by people who turned into pumas, but he tried not to do it without warning her first.

The shift complete, he was about to walk through the thick foliage that surrounded his private garden when a male appeared from the shadows. One that always seemed to be spying on his ass as of late.

"You have a shit-eating grin on your face," Hiss drawled. "I'm assuming that your female has decided you're not the enemy?"

Blade arched a brow. Did he have a shit-eating grin? Probably.

It'd been attached to his lips since he'd claimed Valli.

"Let's just say that I'm enjoying the process of convincing her that I'm one of the good guys."

Hiss nodded. "And the cub?"

Warmth filled his heart. It happened each time he thought of the child growing in Valli's belly. How could he be this lucky?

"Healthy, thank the Goddess."

Hiss reached out to grasp his shoulder. "I'm happy for you, Blade. I truly am," he said, sincerity glowing in his eyes. "You'll discover a mate can soothe wounds you thought would never heal."

Mate. The word whispered through Blade's mind, touching a raw nerve that he'd been trying hard to pretend didn't exist. His smile faded.

"Thanks."

Hiss stilled, his grip tightening on Blade's shoulder. "What's wrong, *mon ami?*"

"Nothing."

Hiss snorted. "Blade, I'm the one person in the Wildlands who will never judge you," he said in wry tones. "Lesson. Fucking. Learned."

Blade hesitated. He didn't want to talk about his inner fears. It was as if speaking them out loud would make them true.

Then he gave a small shake of his head. Maybe talking with Hiss would help alleviate the unease that felt like a lead ball in the pit of his stomach.

"I know that I can stir Valli's passions," he said.

Hiss studied him with an unwavering gaze. "A good start."

"A *great* start," Blade corrected. Just the memory of Valli's lips skimming down his body last night was enough to send jolts of white-hot pleasure through him. "And I know that she's devoted to our child," he continued. More than once he'd watched as Valli had touched her swelling stomach, her face soft with an expression that belonged solely to a mother.

Hiss hesitated, as if wondering why Blade wasn't dancing with joy. Then his gaze flickered toward the nearby cottage before returning to Blade.

"But you're not certain she's devoted to you?" he at last surmised.

Blade clenched his jaw. He was right. Speaking the words out loud did make them worse.

"How can you be sure with a human?" he demanded. "Our people are driven by a mating instinct. We know beyond a shadow of a doubt that we belong together."

He didn't add that he'd been desperately waiting for some sign that Valli had committed herself fully to him. Even he knew he was being idiotic.

After all, what sign could she show him?

Writing him a sappy love song? Tattooing his name on her ass?

Still, it was just so...frustrating.

If she was a Pantera, he'd be able to sense if she'd given herself to the mating. But with a human there was nothing tangible to hold onto. And worse, he sensed that she was keeping a distance between them.

Not physically. She was as passionate as he could ever desire. But there was a part of her that remained elusively out of reach.

It was why he'd never used the word "mate" to her. Even though every time she kissed him, touched him...every time he was inside of her or fuck, just holding her hand as they watched the sunset on the porch, he'd wanted to.

"Humans can be just as loyal." Hiss broke into his dark thoughts. "We've seen that with our own eyes."

It was true. Lately the Pantera had brought many humans into the Wildlands. They had proven to be devoted mates and treasured assets to the pack.

"Yes." He spoke his worse fear. "I just feel like she's holding something back from me."

"Give her time," Hiss commanded. "She's been through hell. She needs time to heal."

Blade grimaced. Logically he knew it'd only been a few days, far too soon for a human female to feel comfortable with the dramatic changes in her life. Especially after all that Valli had endured.

But logic had nothing to do with a male who was eager to mate.

"My cat doesn't want to be patient," he muttered.

Hiss dropped his hand and stepped back, a small smile curving his lips.

"Then be a man until she's ready for your beast," he said.

Blade scowled, watching as Hiss turned and sauntered down the trail.

Be a man? What the hell was that supposed to mean?

Growling deep in his throat, Blade resisted the urge to dismiss the words. Maybe Hiss was right. Being in the Wildlands meant that his cat was much closer to the surface than when he was moving around in the outside world. Perhaps his female needed to know that he could be human as well.

So what did human males do to win the hearts of their females?

A slow smile curved his lips.

Romance.

Ah, yes...

A candlelit dinner. Flowers. Soft music so he could hold her close as they danced.

Yes. He would create a night that would sweep her off her feet. And then he would get down on one knee as a *man* would do, and ask her to be his mate.

But for that, he was going to need help.

Pivoting on his heel, he shifted back into his cat and took off through the trees and back to the communal center.

Chapter 9

Valli had barely waited for Blade to leave that morning before she was pulling on her clothes and heading out of the cottage.

She wasn't trying to be sneaky. At least not deliberately. But after another night of intense, overwhelming passion, she had a desperate need to clear her head.

Blade might be a Diplomat, but he wasn't subtle about what he desired for his future. He wanted her, and the baby she carried, in his home. In the Wildlands. Forever and ever.

A part of her was overjoyed by his steadfast affection. She knew to the very depths of her soul that this male would always be at her side. Always devoted to her and their child.

What more could any woman ask for?

But she'd been raised by someone who'd taught her that every relationship, no matter how bright and shiny in the beginning, was destined to crash and burn. It was going to take time for her to fully trust Blade.

And herself.

And while she adored the small cottage surrounded by lush vegetation, she had a sudden urge to be out of the Wildlands, where she could consider the abrupt changes in her life without Blade, or the potent, irresistible and highly addictive attraction between them, clouding her mind.

Reaching the edge of the wetlands, she stepped through the magical barrier that surrounded the Pantera homeland and started walking down the dirt road. Blade had told her that there was a small town called La

Pierre not far away. She could look around, perhaps find a store to buy a few personal items, and…

Her meandering thoughts were interrupted as the sound of an approaching car shattered the silence. With a frown, Valli moved to the side of the road, a shiver racing over her body. Although the sun had crested the horizon, now that she was out of the Wildlands, there was a sharp breeze that cut easily through her light sweater.

Her frown deepened and her heart started to pound in her chest as the midsize car rounded the curve, and then abruptly skidded to a halt only a few feet from her.

Fast and terrifying, the door was shoved open and the driver leapt out of the vehicle and hurried toward her.

"Valli?" The man reached out to grasp her hands, his face wreathed with a wide smile. "Oh, thank God."

Valli blinked in shock, barely aware the man was tugging her firmly toward the nearby car.

"Dr. Richards?" she muttered, trying to wrap her brain around his sudden appearance.

"Scott," he firmly corrected.

She shook her head. "What are you doing here?"

He led her around the hood of the vehicle and pulled open the passenger door. "I was looking for you."

"Why?"

"I was in the restaurant when you disappeared." He gave her a light push, knocking her off balance so she fell into the seat. Still dazed, she allowed him to tuck her legs into the car. "You ran out the back door, remember? You weren't feeling well."

"Oh," she breathed, genuine regret and deep guilt slicing through her. She'd been so focused on Blade and learning the truth of what had happened to her in the clinic that she hadn't made that call to Fran. How could she have been so thoughtless?

The truth was, she'd spent most of her life without anyone giving a damn about her. It was hard to remember that she was no longer alone.

Scott closed her door and hurried around the car to slide into the driver's seat.

"Fran was hysterical," he said, reaching across to buckle her seatbelt before he was putting the car in gear.

"I'm so sorry." She bit her bottom lip. "I didn't mean to worry anyone."

He sent her a reassuring glance even as he pressed on the gas and drove down the narrow road.

"We know it wasn't your fault," he said.

Valli studied him in confusion. The shock of seeing him was starting to wane, and urgent questions were taking shape inside her mind. Like how had he found her at this remote location?

"How exactly do you know it's not my fault?" she asked cautiously.

"Well, when you didn't return after your walk, Fran went to look for you." His fingers tightened on the steering wheel until his knuckles turned white. "She saw you being carried away by that animal."

Valli felt a blast of fury at the man's insult. Then she grimaced. Hadn't she called Blade an animal before she'd actually been forced to get to know him?

She needed to focus, get answers. She needed to know what the man was doing at the Wildlands.

"How did Fran know the man was a Pantera?"

He stilled for a second, then forced a shrug. "She could tell by the way he moved."

That didn't sound right. If it was true, the older woman was clearly more observant than Valli. Until she'd been surrounded by Pantera, she hadn't really noticed their fluid grace. They just looked like tall, muscular males. And females.

"That still doesn't explain what you're doing here," she pressed.

He turned onto a paved road, pressing harder on the gas pedal as they picked up speed.

A dark thread of unease wove its way through Valli.

"I would think that was obvious," he said. "I had to make sure you were okay."

No. It wasn't obvious at all. In fact, she couldn't imagine how or why the small-town doctor would be driving down that particular road at that particular time.

Something cold drifted up her spine and she reached for the door handle.

"You followed us to the Wildlands, didn't you?" she accused.

"Not exactly," he said. "Fran came back to the restaurant screaming that you'd been kidnapped by an animal. Of course I rushed to try and stop him, but you'd disappeared into thin air."

Anxiety was racing through her now, and she was distantly aware that they were heading north at a pace that had to be way over the speed limit. Were they going back to Bonne? Or was something else going on here?

"He didn't kidnap me," she said, trying to push him into giving her as much information as possible. "I fainted. He was just trying to help me."

Scott made a sound of disbelief. "That's not what Fran told me. She was certain you were in danger, so I decided to come to where the Pantera keep themselves hidden and see if they could help me find you." His profile was tight with anger. "I had no idea that it was impossible to get through the barriers of the swamp. Or that the local people would be so uncooperative."

For a brief second, Valli wondered if this man's motives were honorable. That he'd dropped everything to try and save her. Done more than her own mother had done when she'd disappeared.

But it just didn't sit right. Not in her mind or in her gut. And yet, both had been wrong before.

"The Pantera have to protect themselves," she told him.

His jaw tightened, as if he was biting back his words. When he finally spoke it was in a tone that he no doubt used to calm hysterical patients.

"I can understand their need for security," he assured her. "But it made it difficult to find out if you were here or not."

"And yet you stayed."

"I wasn't leaving until I learned what happened to you." He turned his head, studying her with an intensity that unnerved her. "I care about you, Valli."

Cared about her? He hardly knew her.

Her heart started pounding again, and she turned her head to look out the passenger window. See where she could maybe get him to stop, head to the bathroom and ditch him once and for all.

But there was no town. The swampy landscape had been replaced with the fertile farmland that framed the Mississippi river. They'd traveled farther than she'd realized.

"Where are we going?" she demanded.

"I'm taking you home," he said with a firm finality. "Where you belong."

So that was his objective? Not checking up on her, seeing if she was all right. But taking her home, like a child. But Bonne wasn't her home. Oh, it'd been a place she'd managed to find a measure of peace. And she'd even been happy there for a time.

But it wasn't...

Home.

With a clarity that was shocking in its intensity, she had the answer to the question that had been plaguing her for the past three days.

She belonged in the Wildlands.

With Blade.

With her mate.

He was her true home.

Valli very nearly whirled on the man beside her and demanded he turn around and take her back. Or, at the very least, drop her off and she'd find her way back. Already there was a faint ache in the center of her heart. As if it physically hurt to be parted from Blade. And what if he came back and she wasn't there? Dammit, she hadn't planned to be gone this long...

But she had to return to Bonne anyway... Get her stuff. And she wanted to say good-bye to Fran in person. The woman had been like a surrogate mother to her.

"Do you have a cell phone I can use?" she asked Scott. She wanted to call Blade—he'd made her memorize his cell number in case she'd needed him in town or something was wrong with the cub—and just let him know she was safe and that she was packing up and coming...home.

But Scott gave her a curt "No" as he locked his gaze on the road as they sped through the morning traffic.

Nerves still skittered within her at his gruff response, but when they pulled onto the main road of Bonne, she breathed a sigh of relief. Okay. She'd just been paranoid with all the worry about Scott. Maybe he was into her or something, had a crush? Or a deep sense of loyalty to Fran. If it was the former, then she'd let him down easily. And if the latter, well, then she'd understand perfectly. She'd do anything for Fran, too. Most everyone in the town would.

As soon as he pulled into the garage that was attached to his clinic, Valli scrambled out. Now that she was here, she needed to find a phone and call Blade ASAP, then she'd pack her bags, say good-bye to Fran, and head home to the Wildlands.

Thankfully unaware that she simply wanted to be away from him, Scott politely led her to the side door that opened directly into a hallway.

"Thank you for caring so much about Fran, Dr. Richards, and thank you for the ride," Valli said, attempting to step around him as he came to a sudden halt.

But he wasn't having it. He turned toward her with a frown. "Where are you going?"

"I want to let Fran know I'm okay," she said. She didn't add she was first going to call the Pantera she loved, then she'd see Fran, gather her things, and get the hell out of town. She had a sneaking suspicion that wouldn't go over well with the overprotective doctor.

Without warning, he grabbed her upper arm and guided her into the nearest exam room.

"You're not going anywhere," he said, his expression suddenly grim.

She stared at him in confusion, her heart jolting in her chest. She couldn't get a clear read with this guy, but she was pretty done with trying. "What the hell are you talking about?"

"I'm going to give you a thorough checkup and I'm not taking no for an answer this time," he said, pointing toward the examination table in the center of the tiled floor. "Make yourself comfortable."

Stepping out of the room, Dr. Richards firmly closed the door behind him.

Chapter 10

In his puma form, Blade was ferocity and liquid speed combined. Leaping over rotted logs and ramming his way through the tangled undergrowth, he headed toward the center of the Wildlands.

Fucking hell. This was entirely his fault.

He should have returned directly to Valli when he was done meeting with Raphael. No. He should never have left the cottage in the first place. Not without her, anyway. He'd been foolish. He didn't need fancy dinners and bouquets of flowers to impress a female.

Even though he'd truly believed she'd have loved it.

But in doing so, he'd wasted over an hour arranging the romantic dinner, only to return home to find that Valli was not there.

At first he'd assumed she'd gone for a walk. Since her arrival, she'd spent a few hours every day strolling through the lush, exotic beauty of the Wildlands, sometimes with his cat beside her. But when he'd decided once again to join her, he quickly discovered that she hadn't headed toward the waterfalls or the pretty grotto that was built in the middle of a nearby marsh. Her scent trailed farther out. In fact, it had led him past the bogs that he'd warned her could be dangerous to a human, and then out of the Wildlands.

An expanding sense of concern had spread through him as he'd stepped through the magical barrier that protected his homeland and instantly transformed into his male form. Valli had never left the cottage without telling him where she was going or having him beside her. And while he'd told her early on that there was a nearby town if she ever wanted to shop or just spend time with other humans, she'd never expressed an interest in going.

Still, it wasn't until he'd realized that her scent simply disappeared when it reached the narrow dirt road that real panic set in.

Calling on his inner cat, he'd run full speed back through the barriers and headed straight for the Headquarters of the Pantera. Valli had been taken. He was going to need help to get her back.

He skirted the edge of the communal center and headed up the steps of the Headquarters that were still under construction after being destroyed by one of Benson's soldiers.

He was so intent on reaching Raphael that he didn't notice the male who was just exiting the double doors.

"What the hell?" Hiss muttered in surprise, bracing himself as Blade nearly rammed him down.

With a surge of magic, Blade shifted back to his human form.

He'd intended to find Raph, but Hiss was even better. No one in the Wildlands knew more about the enemy.

Reaching out, he grasped Hiss by the shoulders. "She's been taken."

Hiss frowned. "Who's been taken?"

"Valli."

Hiss stilled, the air prickling with the heat of his cat. "Tell me what's happened."

Blade was forced to take a deep breath. His panic was threatening to overwhelm him, something he couldn't let happen. Not when Valli needed him the most.

"I returned to the cottage and she was gone. No messages, no phone call."

Hiss blinked, clearly puzzled by his explanation. "That doesn't mean anything happened to her. She could be out exploring the Wildlands."

Blade gave a sharp shake of his head. "I followed her trail to the road leading into La Pierre."

Hiss remained unconvinced. "Surely she's allowed to come and go as she pleases, isn't she?"

"Of course she is," Blade snapped.

"Then let her have some space, *mon ami*," Hiss urged in gentle tones, clearly assuming that Blade was simply being an over-possessive male. "An hour or so in town and she'll be ready to come home to you. She's not wanted by anyone. Not in any danger."

Blade released a frustrated growl. "You don't understand. She's disappeared."

"From La Pierre?"

"She never made it there."

Hiss was once again on alert, his expression tightening. "Explain."

"I followed her scent to the road and then it just vanished."

Hiss took a moment to consider the possibilities. "She must have gotten into a vehicle."

"Or more likely forced into a vehicle."

Hiss held his gaze. "Could you detect any sign of a struggle?"

Blade jerked as if he'd been struck. Hell, the words were worse than a physical blow. The male had managed to touch a nerve that was brutally raw.

Dropping his hands, he took a step back. "She didn't leave me," he rasped, a sick fear rolling through his stomach. "Not willingly."

Perhaps sensing that Blade was at a snapping point, Hiss lifted a hand.

"Okay. Let's check the surveillance videos," he said in soothing tones. "They'll show us what happened."

Blade gave a short nod, allowing the male to lead him through one of the double doors into the massive room that would eventually be a reception area, but for now was being used by the Geeks to monitor the numerous computers that were set on long tables.

Once they realized that there were humans out in the world kidnapping and abusing Pantera, they'd poured a massive amount of resources into tracking down their enemies. Magic was all well and good, but nothing replaced Pentagon-grade technology. And as an added bonus, they'd installed a kick-ass surveillance system that kept constant watch on the perimeter of their homeland.

Ignoring the questioning looks, Hiss and Blade crossed toward a shadowed corner. It was close enough to noon for many of the Geeks to be with their families to share lunch, which meant it was easy to find a couple computers that weren't being used.

Hiss sat down on a swivel chair and typed in his password. Blade didn't protest. He was a Suit, not a Geek, which meant he was unfamiliar with the security system.

"What area did she leave the Wildlands?" Hiss demanded, tapping on the keyboard to bring up images from the various cameras.

"The southern quadrant," Blade said. "Near the bogs."

Hiss leaned forward, concentrating on the monitor as he pulled up the video and then pressed the button that would reset it to early that morning. Then, putting the video back in motion, they watched in silence as the dawn chased away the shadows and the landscape was washed in gold.

The minutes passed, stretching Blade's patience until he thought he might snap. At last they could see the bushes that marked the boundary of the Wildlands being pushed aside and a slender female step into view of the camera.

Blade's heart twitched at the sight of her. It'd only been a few hours, but already he felt as if he had a hole in his soul, one that would only be healed when Valli was home.

And in his arms.

"There she is," Hiss murmured.

Blade watched as she hesitantly walked toward the road, as if she was inwardly debating what she wanted to do. Then her head turned, as if she was startled by a sudden noise.

"There's a car approaching."

They both leaned even closer to the screen, watching as a man stopped the vehicle and stepped out to walk directly toward Valli.

"Do you recognize him?" Hiss asked.

Blade furrowed his brow. The man's lack of grace proved he was a human. He was average height and weight, with no distinguishable features. He looked remarkably like a hundred other humans. But Blade had a talent for remembering faces, even the most mundane ones. He would know if he'd seen the man before.

"No."

His hands clenched as the stranger reached out to grab Valli.

"It doesn't look like she's fighting him," Hiss pointed out in wary tones as Valli allowed herself to be urged into the passenger seat of the car.

He should be wary.

Inside Blade, his cat was roaring with fury, thrashing against his skin in an effort to be released so it could hunt down the man and kill him.

His male half wasn't any happier, but he wasn't going to give in to mindless rage. Until he knew exactly what had happened to Valli, he was focused on tracking her down and bringing her back to the Wildlands.

"He might have threatened to hurt her if she tried to get away," he said, a sharp edge in his voice. "She would've done anything to protect our child."

"True," Hiss hastily agreed. "And she doesn't look particularly happy."

Blade pointed toward the monitor. "Can you zoom in on the front of the car?"

"Hold on." Hiss did more tapping on the keyboard and the screen was filled with the chrome grill and bumper.

A grim smile touched Blade's lips as he took a seat at the computer next to Hiss. He didn't know much about the security system, but he was an expert spy. Being a Diplomat meant knowing everything possible about the people who could be an asset or a threat to his people.

He quickly logged into the system and typed in the car's license number. He had several backdoors into government databases, which made it easy enough to identify the owner of the vehicle.

"Shit," he breathed as the information popped up on the screen.

Hiss moved his chair to glance at Blade's computer. "What did you find?"

"The vehicle belongs to Dr. Scott Richards."

"Should I recognize the name?" Hiss demanded.

"He's the doctor who convinced Valli to go to the clinic in Baton Rouge."

"Oh, fuck me, no." Hiss slammed his hand on the table. "He must work for Benson."

Blade shoved himself out of his chair. "Come on."

"Where are we going?" Hiss asked as Blade led him toward the door.

"To have a word with the good doctor."

"To have a word with him or to kill him?" Hiss asked as he lengthened his strides to keep up with Blade.

"First the words, and then the killing," Blade said, then he growled, low and feral. "On second thought, maybe just the killing. Words are overrated."

Chapter 11

Valli felt on edge and slightly ridiculous as she cautiously opened the door of the examination room and peeked into the hall. She didn't know what was up with Scott, if he was actually attempting to hold her against her will or what. She didn't think he had any ill will toward her... Why in the world would he? But his overwhelming concern for her, and no doubt some level of romantic crush, was highly obnoxious and downright creepy.

Thing was, though, she didn't want to have a protracted argument about either issue. Not when she was anxious to get her things and call Blade to come and get her.

Avoidance, it is.

Hating herself a little for sneaking away and not just telling the annoying doctor it was her body and she'd get it checked when she wanted and with whom, Valli quietly entered the hallway and crossed to the side exit. She paused to ensure she wasn't being followed, then with a burst of speed, she darted across the street and down the block. Five minutes later, she was pulling open the glass door of the restaurant and skidding to a halt in the center of the dining room.

Instantly she felt better and, strangely, safer. She breathed deeply of the familiar scents of warm bread and freshly baked pies as she heard the pitter-patter of Fran hurrying out of the kitchen.

"Valli," the woman breathed, eyes going wide as she moved forward, wiping the flour off her hands. "Oh, lordie. Oh, hun. I've been so worried."

Valli's heart squeezed with both guilt and affection. She hated that she'd made this woman upset. This woman who'd done nothing but care for her. "I'm fine," she assured her.

Eyes soft now, Fran reached up to pat Valli's cheek. "I'll judge that for myself," she said in her classic gruff tone.

After she'd looked her over for a solid minute, the older women left her side and scurried toward the door. She turned the sign to *Closed* and clicked the bolt into place. "Now, we won't be disturbed." Turning, she waved Valli to follow her. "Have a seat and let me get you a slice of pecan pie. I want to hear everything that's been going on."

"I'm really not hungry," Valli said, even as she slid into one of the chairs in the small dining room. She needed to call Blade, even just to let him know she was all right.

"Nonsense," Fran protested, fluttering in and back out of the kitchen with an energy that made Valli's head spin. "Everyone is hungry for my pie."

Valli swallowed a sigh and grinned. Fran wouldn't be happy until she'd eaten her pie.

"I'm sorry if I worried you," Valli said, her mouth watering as Fran set the plate in front of her, along with a large glass of cold milk. She'd lied when she said she wasn't hungry. It'd been a long time since breakfast. She'd just been so anxious to get home, back to Blade. "I didn't consider the fact that I just disappeared. I wasn't thinking."

Fran took a seat across the table, studying Valli with a searching gaze, as if assuring herself that Valli was unharmed by her recent adventure.

"I'll tell you it gave me a right start to see that creature carrying you away," the older woman admitted. "What was he doing back there?"

Valli lowered her head as she took a large bite of pie. She didn't want Fran to see her expression.

"Looking for me."

Her eyes widened. "You know him?"

Valli took another bite of pie and then a drink of milk before answering. "It's a long story."

No doubt sensing Valli's unwillingness to discuss Blade, Fran curbed the subject, folded her hands in her lap and cleared her throat.

"Well, I didn't know what to do, but Dr. Richards said that he would go to the Wildlands and demand that you be returned to us."

Valli grimaced as she pushed aside her half-eaten pie and drank the last of the milk. She felt a slight twinge of guilt for sneaking away from Scott. Creepy and crushing on her aside, he had spent days trying to find her, get her back to Fran.

"Yes, he's the one who brought me back to Bonne," she admitted.

Fran smiled. A smug, satisfied smile. "Ah, I knew I could depend on him," she murmured. "He's a fine man."

Valli gave an obligatory nod of agreement, then instantly wished she hadn't. Her head suddenly felt as if it was too heavy for her neck. And worse, her brain was starting to spin.

"He clearly cares about you a lot," Valli said, trying to shake off the strange sensations.

"And you," Fran said, pulling her phone from the pocket of her apron. "But you're not keen on him, are you?"

"No, not at all," Valli agreed, her heart missing a beat at the thought of Blade. "I have someone waiting for me."

Fran curled her lips. "One of those animals?"

"He's not—" Valli bit off her words, her head pulsing strangely. She wasn't going to waste her time arguing. She wanted to be back in the Wildlands with her man. Her mate. The father of her child. "Doesn't matter. I have to pack my things."

"No need. I've already boxed them up," Fran told her.

"You did?" Valli said in surprise, though her voice sounded oddly weak and raspy. Had the older woman assumed she wasn't coming back? Maybe she'd already hired a new waitress and rented out the room upstairs.

"Yes. You can take them with you." Fran lifted her phone and spoke to some unseen listener. "She's here. Hurry up."

Valli shoved herself upright, gritting her teeth as her dizziness intensified. What the hell was wrong with her? Was this one of the same old dizzy spells she'd had before she left?

"Who was that?" she demanded, apprehension snaking down her spine.

That feeling...the one she'd had in the car, and—damn her—in the clinic...hummed inside of her. Something wasn't right. She wasn't right. And her child...

"My contact with Benson Enterprises," Fran said simply. "He's promised me a very lucrative payment to hand over you and that abomination you're cooking in there."

Valli blinked, her breath stalled inside her lungs. She blinked again.

Fran looked the same, her long red hair coiled into a knot at the back of her head, her hooked nose and bright brown eyes.

But it was as if Valli was seeing her for the first time.

She shook her woozy head. "No, Fran..."

"Now I know it's a little premature," she went on as if nothing had changed between them, as if what she was saying was the sanest thing in the world. "I'd hoped to wait until after you'd given birth. I'm sure I could have demanded an even higher price. But now that the animals know where you live, I can't take the risk that they might come looking for you."

Valli lifted a hand to her head. It was buzzing now, like a hundred flies were inside of it. She couldn't think clearly. Couldn't move.

"I don't understand." The words came out in a whisper.

The older woman rose to her feet, a smirk twisting her lips.

"Of course you don't," she said in mocking tones. "Poor, pathetic Valli. So desperate for a mother to love her."

Valli grabbed the back of the chair, her knees feeling weak. The baby. Her cub...

"How do you..." she struggled. "How do you know Benson?"

Fran shrugged. "He gave me the money to start this restaurant with the understanding I would regularly send him young women he can use for his experimentations."

Oh, God. Her heart dropped into the floor. How was this possible? And how could she have been so stupid? Hadn't life taught her that no one could be trusted?

No one but Blade.

She had to move, get out, run...before they came... She had to get home to Blade.

But nothing was working. Not her mind or her legs. Fran had drugged her with that goddamned pie and Blade didn't know where she was.

"Fran, please don't do this," she rasped, trying anything she could...her tongue so thick that the words came out slurred. "I know you cared about me."

Fran dropped her phone on the table and untied her apron, as if she was preparing for company.

The thought made Valli's stomach cramp with terror.

"Once a year I would ride the bus around the state, waiting to find a suitable test subject," Fran explained. "They were specific in their needs. She had to be young, fertile, and without family ties." She flicked a dismissive glance over Valli. "You were perfect."

Perfect?

Struggling to stay upright, Valli shuddered. She'd been drugged, forcibly inseminated, and hypnotized into believing that she'd been raped by the father of her child. And now, this piece of shit she'd allowed herself to believe in and trust was trying to send her back. For what? To be a lab rat? To have her child taken from her?

"Why didn't you take me straight to the clinic?" she demanded, pushing the woman to talk so she could think, try to figure a way out.

"You had to be given hormones before the actual procedure. They expected me to ensure you were properly prepared." Fran heaved a sigh, as if she'd been unbearably exhausted by the process of betraying a young, innocent woman.

Forcing her gaze around the room for anything she could use as a weapon—butter knives, glasses—Valli lifted a shaky hand to press it against the soft swell of her stomach. Inside, her baby slept with peaceful oblivion.

"I didn't take any hormones," she protested.

Fran shrugged. "Course you did, hon. I slipped them into your evening tea."

God. She'd been so epically stupid. She'd actually looked forward to the nightly tea and scones she'd shared with this woman.

And all the time Fran was simply priming her to become a caged lab rat.

She needed to get to the kitchen where the butcher knives were kept. Maybe it was being in the Wildlands with the pumas and their Hunter nature, maybe it was the puma she carried inside of her...but she'd changed. In just a few days, she'd changed. Sinking a fierce, sharp blade into this woman's heart sounded like bliss.

"So that's what made me sick and dizzy," Valli choked out, using all her remaining energy to inch toward the next table.

"No." Fran chuckled, looking exceptionally pleased with herself. "That was a special ingredient that I baked into your scones. Once you were close to being finished with the hormone treatment, I had to get you to the client. The easiest way was to convince you that you were dying. You would not only be eager to go to Baton Rouge, but you would let the doctors do whatever they wanted."

Valli swayed, her knees close to buckling. She grabbed onto the back of the chair at the next table. She had to make her move quickly if she was really going to have any chance of escaping.

"How many others?" she abruptly demanded, releasing her hold on the chair as she gathered her fading strength. The kitchen was close. She could do it. But she'd have to run.

Fran lifted a puzzled brow. "What?"

"How many women did you send to the clinic?"

"Oh. Nine. Maybe ten. But none of them got pregnant." Fran's smile widened with blatant anticipation. "You, my dear, are my ticket to retirement."

The woman's complete lack of regret sent a burst of fury through Valli, giving her the strength she needed. But not to run away. The Pantera were inside of her now. They didn't run from their enemies.

They attacked.

"And you are one evil fucking bitch!" she screamed before leaping forward to grab the woman by her neck and slam her against the nearby counter.

Chapter 12

Blade peered around the edge of the fence, studying the squat brick building with frosted glass. The sign in the front had assured him that this was Dr. Scott Richard's Medical Facility. And while he couldn't see any cars in the parking lot, he could smell a human inside.

As well as Valli's lingering scent.

His cat roared in triumph.

When he'd realized who'd taken his female, he'd thought of nothing but getting to her. It had been Hiss who'd insisted that they inform Raphael what had happened and that they were leaving to rescue Valli and bring her home.

Not surprisingly, the leader had demanded that he be in on the hunt, along with Jean-Baptiste, who took it as a personal insult that a human had captured one of his patients.

"You keep a watch out here," Blade commanded Hiss, who was standing at his side with a handgun aimed at the back door.

Although they were stronger and faster than any human even when they couldn't shift, most Hunters were trained to use traditional weapons.

It was easier to shoot a man in the heart than rip off his head, even if it wasn't nearly as satisfying.

He took a step forward, only to be brought to a halt as Hiss reached out to grab his arm.

"Wait."

Blade turned his head to scowl at the male. "For what?"

Hiss nodded toward the building. "This could be a trap. We've both been burned before. I prefer not to repeat the experience."

"My mate is in danger." Blade wrenched his arm free of his friend's grip. "I don't give a shit if it's a trap or not."

Hiss made a sound of frustration. "At least give Raph and Jean-Baptiste a chance to get into place before you go charging in there like a cowboy."

The two males were doing a sweep of the nearby streets to search for any signs of Benson's soldiers.

"Cowboys don't charge," he corrected his companion. "They gallop to the rescue."

"Yeah, well…shit." Hiss's words echoed behind Blade as he vaulted over the fence and headed directly to the nearby door.

With a speed that would make him all but invisible to the casual observer, Blade was across the parking lot and shoving open the back door. He paused long enough to sniff the air, then he was jogging down the hall to enter a large office that was stuffed with shelves, filing cabinets, and stacks of X-rays on a lighted table.

At the entrance, a man shoved himself to his feet, rounding the desk with an impatient scowl.

"Can I help you?"

His last word came out in a painful grunt as Blade grabbed him by the lapels of his white lab coat and lifted him off the ground before he slammed him against a nearby bookshelf.

"Where is she?" he growled.

The man struggled to suck air back into his lungs, his face flushing with outrage.

"What are you doing?" he rasped, futilely struggling. "Let me go."

Blade leaned forward, allowing his cat to glow in his eyes. "Where. Is. She."

The doctor coughed, his eyes darkening with fear as he seemed to understand just who he was dealing with and why he was there.

"You're a beast."

Blade curled back his lips, the air sizzling and popping around him. Not even the most oblivious human could fail to sense his power. "You have no idea."

With a visible effort, the doctor tried to hide his fear behind a brittle pretense of defiance.

"You might be able to act like a savage in your swamps, but in civilized society we have laws," he blustered. "Leave Bonne or I'll call the cops and have you arrested."

"I'm not asking again." Blade tightened his grip. He couldn't sense any other humans, but that didn't mean they weren't hiding near enough that they could ambush him while he was distracted. "Give me Valli."

The man's face paled to a sickly white, but he gamely continued to struggle.

"No." His voice was hoarse. "She just escaped from you. I'm not handing her back to her kidnapper."

Blade hissed, his eyes narrowing with rage. "You're the one who's holding her captive."

The man blinked, acting like he was offended by Blade's accusation.

"Me?" He flailed his legs, as if he could actually hurt Blade with a kick to his shin. "I saved her when she escaped from the Wildlands. She was frantic to come home."

The kick didn't hurt, but his words hit Blade with the force of a sledgehammer.

He sucked in a sharp breath, even as his heart whispered that Valli would never leave him. Not willingly.

"Liar," he growled. "You're working with Benson."

More blinking. The fucker looked like a drunk owl.

"Who?"

Blade gave him another slam against the bookcase. "Don't act stupid."

A fine layer of sweat covered the doctor's face. No doubt he was starting to realize that Blade didn't play by his rules. He was ready, willing, and fully capable of killing him.

"I don't know any Benson."

Blade released a low snarl. Did he really think he could lie his way out of this? Or was he just stalling for time? Maybe hoping his friends would arrive and save him from the crazed Pantera.

"Valli told me that you were the one who sent her to the clinic."

"Oh. You mean Benson Clinic?" He didn't wait for Blade to respond. "She was ill. I couldn't cure her, so of course I sent her to doctors who might be capable of discovering what was wrong with her," he said in defensive tones.

Blade's nose flared, the memories of the clinic pounding through him.

The darkness. The pain. The drugged horror on Valli's face as they'd violated her...

"You sent her to become a lab rat for a megalomaniac billionaire who uses vulnerable women to create his vision of super-soldiers," he accused.

He abruptly released his hold on the man, dropping him to the ground. It was that or pounding him against the shelf until he was a bloody corpse.

For now, he needed the bastard alive.

The doctor awkwardly stumbled before he managed to regain his balance. Lifting his hand, he wiped the sweat from his brow.

"What?" He shook his head. "No. That's not possible."

Blade slammed his fist into the wall, punching a hole through the drywall.

"Don't try to act innocent. The clinic is a front for human and Pantera experimentation. I was held as a prisoner there."

The doctor squeaked and pressed himself against the bookshelf.

"I was told it was a cutting-edge research facility that specialized in rare illnesses. I would never have... I care about Valli. I'd hoped..."

Blade clenched his jaw. The man might be able to pretend to be confused, but there was no way he could create his panicky scent that made Blade's nose wrinkle.

Dammit. Had Dr. Richards been another puppet who'd been used by Benson to further his own goals?

If so, then who'd been pulling his strings?

"Who told you that?" he demanded.

"Fran Meyer," the doctor confessed without hesitation. "She had a family member who went there when no one else could help him." He waved a trembling hand toward his cluttered desk. "I have a pamphlet and everything."

"Fran." The name teased at the edge of his memory. "The woman who invited Valli to Bonne?" He at last managed to recall the story that Valli had told him about her time of roaming around the country and how she'd finally settled down after meeting a woman who'd offered her a home and steady employment.

The doctor nodded. "I think they met on the bus and got to talking. Fran is a good woman. She couldn't have done anything. Not to Valli."

Shit. They needed to track down Fran before she could flee. But first he wanted to hold his mate in his arms.

"Where's Valli?" he demanded. He could catch her scent, but it seemed distant.

"This way. I was just trying to help her. I thought she'd been kidnapped."

Careful to keep his movements slow, as if smart enough to realize that it wouldn't take much for Blade to consider him a threat, he headed toward the door. Blade followed close behind, a sudden heat brushing through the air as he heard the front door being pushed open.

Raphael and Jean-Baptiste were in the building.

Seemingly unaware that he was surrounded, the doctor hurried down the hallway, pushing open the last door.

He came to a sharp halt, and Blade barely stopped in time to keep from ramming into him.

"What are you doing?" Blade snapped.

The doctor stepped to the side, revealing the empty room. "She's gone."

Chapter 13

With every shred of energy and focus she could muster, Valli squeezed the woman's neck. It wasn't so much an attempt to kill her but to make her pass out. Of course, if Fran happened to die in the process, Valli wouldn't shed a tear.

Hell, she might throw a party.

After she got the hell out of Bonne, that is.

"I think...you of all people—" Fran gasped, her face starting to turn purple. "—would understand, Valli."

"Understand what?" Valli clenched her teeth, battling back the massive dizziness and the encroaching darkness. She suspected she'd already be unconscious if it wasn't for the Pantera blood she'd been given in the clinic. Or maybe it was her Pantera child. Granted, neither had turned her into Wonder Woman, but it did give her a few perks. "That you're willing to sell the girls who trust you?"

Fran bent backward over the counter in an attempt to break Valli's grim grip.

"It's a cruel world," she grunted, straining. "Especially for a woman on her own. I had to do..." She gasped again. "I had to do whatever was necessary to survive."

"Does that bullshit excuse allow you to sleep at night?" Valli demanded in disgusted tones.

Without warning, the woman suddenly jerked to the side, her hand reaching out to grasp a small steak knife that was on the countertop.

How had she missed seeing that? Valli cursed and jumped backward, but not before the razor-sharp blade sliced through the skin of her upper arm.

"I sleep just fine," Fran assured her with a smirking smile. "And I'll sleep even better once I have my condo on the beach."

Gritting her teeth, Valli tried unsuccessfully to ignore the wound. It wasn't deep, but it was crazy painful. And the blood dripping down her arm wasn't helping. She was already weak.

Fran was holding the knife like a pro, like someone who cut meat for a living. Valli backed away, looking for an opening. It was now more vital than ever that she disable the woman so she could get out of the diner.

"If something happens to me you can forget the money and condo," she warned the woman. "Blade will hunt you down and rip out your heart."

"I'm not afraid of those animals," the woman spat out.

"Then you're even more stupid than I thought."

Not giving herself time to think of the danger, Valli leaped forward, a strange growl rumbling in her throat. Apparently she had more Pantera blood in her veins than she'd realized.

Thank you, my cub.

No longer young and spry, Fran lost her balance and fell on her ass, her feet churning as she scuttled into the corner. Just like a cockroach.

"Don't be foolish, Valli." She waved the knife. "I don't want to hurt you."

Valli continued forward, no fear, just feral anger. "Of course not. I'm your cash cow, aren't I?"

Fran drew back deeper into the corner, her fist tight around the blade. "Stay back."

"I'll die before I let anyone take my child or use it as a weapon." Valli took another step, judging the distance. She didn't intend to get cut again.

Genuine fear flared over Fran's pale face. She was beginning to realize she was trapped with a woman who was not only willing to fight back, but kill to protect herself and her baby.

"No!" she cried out. "Just go. Please…go!"

But it was too late. Valli lunged forward, feinting to the left. As she'd hoped, Fran tried slashing the knife in a wild motion. Adrenaline running high, Valli jumped to the side, curling her hand into a fist. Then, begging everything within her to grant her that last ounce of strength, she swung her arm to land a direct punch to Fran's chin.

A shock of pain instantly ran up her arm. Such a violent impact. But Valli barely noticed. Because pleasure was there too. She watched in utter satisfaction as the woman's eyes rolled to the back of her head and she slumped to the side.

Knocked out cold.

Knife rolling from her limp fist to the floor.

Breathing a little labored, flies still buzzing in her head, Valli grinned. Fuck yeah! Blade was right. She did have one hell of a right hook.

Unable to take the time to properly gloat, Valli turned toward the back door. The movement was enough to make her stumble as her knees threatened to buckle.

Adrenaline gone.

Gritting her teeth, she reached out to lay her hand against the wall. It was the only thing keeping her upright as she took one cautious step after another. She was fading fast. She'd used up everything.

After what seemed to be an eternity, she finally reached the exit. But even then she struggled to grab the knob with enough strength to turn it and push the door open.

Go. You've got to go.

They're still coming...for you, for the cub...

A brisk breeze tugged at her hair as she stumbled out of the diner. She reached up to push it out of her face, belatedly noticing the two men who were crawling out of a black SUV.

Oh...shit...

Benson's men.

A cry broke from her lips. She was too late.

But the defeatist thought in her head had barely enough time to form, because coming around the side of the building was the wonderful, terrifying sound of a Pantera's roar.

Her heart leapt.

Benson's goons turned in shock, both of them reaching for the handguns they had strapped to their hips.

Feeling as if she was in a dream, Valli watched as Blade zoomed forward. He moved so fast he was almost a blur, reaching the men before they could squeeze off a shot.

He grabbed the first one by the head, jerking it to the side. Valli heard the snap, crackle, pop of the man's neck breaking, followed by a dull thud as Blade dropped him to the ground, then magically whirled back around to grab the gun out of the second man's hand.

He was magnificent.

After witnessing that, the second man gaped at him in horror, not even trying to escape as Blade lifted his arm and used the butt of the gun to smash in the side of the man's head. It squashed like a pumpkin, and he slowly tumbled on top of his dead companion.

Only then did Blade turn to glance toward Valli.

She managed a weak smile. He was fierce and formidable and would always have her back.

Her man.

Her warrior.

Her beloved mate.

The father of her cub.

And then she gave in to both the exhaustion and the drugs, and the world went dark.

Chapter 14

Valli came awake slowly.

Her eyes opening first, then her mind processing second.

White walls, closet, pale blue blanket, soft sheets, and the bayou-scented breeze coming in through the open window.

Her heart warmed and her pulsed slowed.

She was home.

Everything rushed back to her: leaving the Wildlands, the doctor, Fran, Benson's goons…and Blade. Her hero.

Something moved on the floor; something was coming to its feet…

No fears rushed over her. That part of her life was gone now. She'd seen and faced betrayal—and in doing so she'd been given the gift of trust. In herself, and in another.

Blade's puma, with its anxious black eyes and massive gold head, padded over to the bedside. Instantly Valli reached for it, her hand stroking its face. Soft fur over hard bone and muscle. Glorious.

With a soft snarl, the beast dropped its head, resting its chin on the mattress near her side.

"I've missed you," she whispered to it, threading her fingers in its thick fur. "So has the cub."

The puma's nostrils flared as it inhaled, and when it caught a scent, its eyes closed and it started to purr.

For Valli, she didn't hesitate or question the beauty of the moment. It just was now. Her life, her reality. And she deserved it. That amazing truth was what she'd finally come to realize.

The Wildlands was pure magic, and as she stroked the beast under her hand, the fur receded and the male emerged.

Clearly, he'd shifted naked and gloriously powerful, because that was how he materialized before her.

"Valli..." He crawled into bed and gathered her in his arms. His eyes raked over her, checking...

"I'm okay," she assured him. "Are you okay?"

He released a weighty breath, but held her close, their heads a few inches apart, eyes locked. "Don't leave me again, *ma chère.*"

"Never."

"I wouldn't be able to continue existing without you."

"And the cub," she added.

"Of course." His brows furrowed as he studied her. "Wait... You don't think... This, you and me, you don't think it's just about the cub?"

She hated herself for the thought, for the moment of emotional weakness, but she couldn't stop herself from expressing it. "I would understand, and it doesn't change anything—"

He had her on her back in seconds, tossing away the blanket. With slow, deliberate hands he removed her clothing. Then he moved down toward her feet.

His eyes on her, he started with her ankles. Soft kisses, gentle bites. "Oh, my beautiful, intelligent, fierce Valli with the killer right hook..."

Her breath caught as he scraped his teeth against the inside of her knee.

"I don't think you fully understand," he whispered, moving up, up until his head was poised between her thighs. "But you must. I love you."

He didn't touch her, didn't lick her, as she was about to beg him to do. His eyes were still clinging to hers.

"And I want you, Valli. Every part of you, but especially your heart." His eyes glistened with happiness. "I'm thrilled and grateful for our cub, you have no idea how much, because it brought us together."

If the heart and body could suddenly become one organ, beating with life and exquisite love, that was what Valli experienced in that moment.

"You're my world," he uttered with deep emotion. "My mate, and my family."

It was a strange thing, family. It wasn't found only in blood—sometimes it wasn't there at all. Sometimes it was found in the hearts and souls of those who were lucky enough to love.

A soft sigh threatened to steal her last thought as Blade lowered his head and spread her wide before him.

But she pulled it back. Because it was important. It was everything.

And be loved in return.

"Oh, my sweet mate," Blade uttered as he lapped at her, circling her sensitive bud with his tongue. "Welcome home."

Home, Valli thought wondrously, as she fisted the sheets and let her male, her mate, take her once again over the edge of reason and into a world of blissful magic.

Finally, home.

* * * *

Also from 1001 Dark Nights and Alexandra Ivy and Laura Wright, discover Rage/Killian and Kayden/Simon.

Sign up for the 1001 Dark Nights Newsletter
and be entered to win a Tiffany Key necklace.

There's a contest every month!

Go to www.1001DarkNights.com to subscribe.

As a bonus, all subscribers will receive a free
1001 Dark Nights story
The First Night
by Lexi Blake & M.J. Rose

Discover 1001 Dark Nights Collection Four

ROCK CHICK REAWAKENING by Kristen Ashley
A Rock Chick Novella

ADORING INK by Carrie Ann Ryan
A Montgomery Ink Novella

SWEET RIVALRY by K. Bromberg

SHADE'S LADY by Joanna Wylde
A Reapers MC Novella

RAZR by Larissa Ione
A Demonica Underworld Novella

ARRANGED by Lexi Blake
A Masters and Mercenaries Novella

TANGLED by Rebecca Zanetti
A Dark Protectors Novella

HOLD ME by J. Kenner
A Stark Ever After Novella

SOMEHOW, SOME WAY by Jennifer Probst
A Billionaire Builders Novella

TOO CLOSE TO CALL by Tessa Bailey
A Romancing the Clarksons Novella

HUNTED by Elisabeth Naughton
An Eternal Guardians Novella

EYES ON YOU by Laura Kaye
A Blasphemy Novella

BLADE by Alexandra Ivy/Laura Wright
A Bayou Heat Novella

DRAGON BURN by Donna Grant
A Dark Kings Novella

TRIPPED OUT by Lorelei James
A Blacktop Cowboys® Novella

STUD FINDER by Lauren Blakely

MIDNIGHT UNLEASHED by Lara Adrian
A Midnight Breed Novella

HALLOW BE THE HAUNT by Heather Graham
A Krewe of Hunters Novella

DIRTY FILTHY FIX by Laurelin Paige
A Fixed Novella

THE BED MATE by Kendall Ryan
A Room Mate Novella

NIGHT GAMES by CD Reiss
A Games Novella

NO RESERVATIONS by Kristen Proby
A Fusion Novella

DAWN OF SURRENDER by Liliana Hart
A MacKenzie Family Novella

Discover 1001 Dark Nights Collection One

FOREVER WICKED by Shayla Black
CRIMSON TWILIGHT by Heather Graham
CAPTURED IN SURRENDER by Liliana Hart
SILENT BITE: A SCANGUARDS WEDDING by Tina Folsom
DUNGEON GAMES by Lexi Blake
AZAGOTH by Larissa Ione
NEED YOU NOW by Lisa Renee Jones
SHOW ME, BABY by Cherise Sinclair
ROPED IN by Lorelei James
TEMPTED BY MIDNIGHT by Lara Adrian
THE FLAME by Christopher Rice
CARESS OF DARKNESS by Julie Kenner

Also from 1001 Dark Nights

TAME ME by J. Kenner

Discover 1001 Dark Nights Collection Two

WICKED WOLF by Carrie Ann Ryan
WHEN IRISH EYES ARE HAUNTING by Heather Graham
EASY WITH YOU by Kristen Proby
MASTER OF FREEDOM by Cherise Sinclair
CARESS OF PLEASURE by Julie Kenner
ADORED by Lexi Blake
HADES by Larissa Ione
RAVAGED by Elisabeth Naughton
DREAM OF YOU by Jennifer L. Armentrout
STRIPPED DOWN by Lorelei James
RAGE/KILLIAN by Alexandra Ivy/Laura Wright
DRAGON KING by Donna Grant
PURE WICKED by Shayla Black
HARD AS STEEL by Laura Kaye
STROKE OF MIDNIGHT by Lara Adrian
ALL HALLOWS EVE by Heather Graham
KISS THE FLAME by Christopher Rice
DARING HER LOVE by Melissa Foster
TEASED by Rebecca Zanetti
THE PROMISE OF SURRENDER by Liliana Hart

Also from 1001 Dark Nights

THE SURRENDER GATE By Christopher Rice
SERVICING THE TARGET By Cherise Sinclair

Discover 1001 Dark Nights Collection Three

About Alexandra Ivy and Laura Wright

Alexandra Ivy is a *New York Times* and *USA Today* bestselling author of the Guardians of Eternity, as well as the Sentinels, Dragons of Eternity and ARES series. After majoring in theatre she decided she prefers to bring her characters to life on paper rather than stage. She lives in Missouri with her family. Visit her website at alexandraivy.com.

New York Times and USA Today bestselling author, Laura Wright is passionate about romantic fiction. Though she has spent most of her life immersed in acting, singing and competitive ballroom dancing, when she found the world of writing and books and endless cups of coffee she knew she was home. Laura is the author of the bestselling Mark of the Vampire series and the USA Today bestselling series, Bayou Heat, which she co-authors with Alexandra Ivy.

Laura lives in Los Angeles with her husband, two young children and three loveable dogs.

Discover More Alexandra Ivy and Laura Wright

Rage/Killian
Bayou Heat Novellas
By Alexandra Ivy and Laura Wright

RAGE

Rage might be an aggressive Hunter by nature, but the gorgeous male has never had a problem charming the females. All except Lucie Gaudet. Of course, the lovely Geek is a born troublemaker, and it was no surprise to Rage when she was kicked out of the Wildlands.

But now the Pantera need a first-class hacker to stop the potential destruction of their people. And it's up to Rage to convince Lucie to help. Can the two forget the past—and their sizzling attraction—to save the Pantera?

KILLIAN

Gorgeous, brutal, aggressive, and *human*, Killian O'Roarke wants only two things: to get rid of the Pantera DNA he's been infected with, and get back to the field. But the decorated Army Ranger never bargained on meeting the woman—the female—of his dreams on his mission to the Wildlands.

Rosalie lost her mate to a human, and now the Hunter despises them all. In fact, she thinks they're good for only one thing: barbeque. But this one she's guarding is testing her beliefs. He is proud and kind, and also knows the pain of loss. But in a time of war between their species, isn't any chance of love destined for destruction?

* * * *

Kayden/Simon
Bayou Heat Novellas
By Alexandra Ivy & Laura Wright

ENEMY TO LOVER:
Kayden is obsessed with revenge after his parents disappeared when he was just a cub. Now the gorgeous Hunter has discovered the man responsible for betraying them - Joshua Ford - and it's time for payback. Beginning with the kidnapping of Joshua's daughter, Bianca. But last thing he expects is to be confronted with the horrifying realization that Bianca is his mate. Will he put revenge before his chance for eternal happiness?

BEAUTY AND THE BEAST

Sexy male model, Simon refuses to give up his exciting life in New York City to return to the slow heat of the Wildlands. For a decade, many Pantera have tried to capture the rogue Diplomat and bring him home, but all have failed. Now it's Tryst's turn. The hard, brilliant, and gorgeous, Hunter is the ultimate tracker. But can the admitted beast-girl of the Wildlands capture her prey without losing her heart in the process?

Pretend You're Safe
By Alexandra Ivy
Coming August 29, 2017

HE SEES YOU

First came the floods. Then came the bodies. The victims—strangled, then buried along the shores of the Mississippi—have finally been unearthed, years after they disappeared. He remembers every satisfying kill... each woman's terror and agony. But there's only one he truly wanted. And fate has brought her within reach again...

HE KNOWS YOU

Jaci Patterson was sixteen when she found the first golden locket on her porch. Inside were a few strands of hair wrapped around a scrap of bloodstained ribbon. Though the "gifts" kept arriving, no one believed her hunch that a serial killer was at work. Now Jaci has returned home... and the nightmare is starting once more.

AND HE'LL NEVER LET YOU GO

Back then, Rylan Cooper was an arrogant deputy sheriff convinced that Jaci was just an attention—seeking teen. It was a fatal mistake. There's a murderer in their midst, someone determined to settle old scores and keep playing a twisted game. And it won't end until Jaci is his forever...

"Alexandra Ivy gives readers a nice balance of romance and suspense in her fast-paced, well-plotted novel." —Kat Martin, *New York Times* bestselling author

* * * *

PROLOGUE

Frank Johnson had endured his fair share of floods. He'd been born and raised on the small farm that butted against the bank of the Mississippi River. Which meant he'd spent the past sixty years watching the muddy waters rise and fall. Sometimes sweeping away crops, cattle, and during one memorable year, the barn that had been built by his great-grandfather.

The levee that'd been built by the Corps of Engineers over a decade ago had provided a measure of security. Not that he'd been happy when they'd come in and scooped up his fertile land to create the barrier. Frank was a typical Midwestern farmer who didn't need the government poking their noses, or bulldozers, into his business. But eventually he'd had to admit it was nice not to have the waters lapping at the back door every time it rained.

But this was no typical rain.

On the first of February the heavens had opened up and six weeks later, the torrential rains continued to pound the small community. The river had become an angry, churning, destructive force as it swept toward the south. Frank watched in resignation as the water had inched closer and closer to the top of the levee. He knew it was only a matter of time before it spilled over the ridge and into his back field.

But when he woke that morning, it wasn't to find the levee had been topped. Nope. It had been busted wide open. As if someone had set off an explosion during the night.

With the resignation of a man who'd lived his entire life dependent on the fickleness of nature, he'd pulled on his coveralls and boots before firing up his old tractor and heading down to see the damage.

Dawn had arrived, but the thick clouds and persistent drizzle shrouded the farm in a strange gloom. Frank pulled the collar of his coveralls up to protect his neck from the chilled breeze, starting to feel like Noah. Had he missed the memo from God that he was supposed to build an ark?

The inane thought had barely formed in his mind when he allowed the tractor to roll to a halt. As expected, his fields had become pools of brown, brackish water. In some places the nasty stuff was waist deep. There were also the usual leaves, branches, and pieces of flotsam that'd been caught in the swirling eddies.

What he hadn't expected was the long, dark object that he spotted floating in the middle of his pasture.

His first thought had been that it was a log. Maybe a piece of lumber torn from a building. But a piece of wood wouldn't make his stomach cramp with a sense of dread, would it?

Climbing off his tractor, he'd reached into his pocket for his cell phone. His unconscious mind had already warned him that whatever the floodwaters had washed onto his land was going to be bad.

And it was.

Really, really bad.

On behalf of 1001 Dark Nights,

Liz Berry and M.J. Rose would like to thank ~

Steve Berry
Doug Scofield
Kim Guidroz
Jillian Stein
InkSlinger PR
Dan Slater
Asha Hossain
Chris Graham
Pamela Jamison
Fedora Chen
Kasi Alexander
Jessica Johns
Dylan Stockton
Richard Blake
BookTrib After Dark
and Simon Lipskar

CPSIA information can be obtained
at www.ICGtesting.com
Printed in the USA
LVOW12s1613231217
560657LV00001B/234/P